WELL PLAYED

Stoke's eyes grew darker. "Ever since I met you, you've haunted me, Atalanta James. When you're not with me, I can't get you out of my head. You're"—he reached up a hand and softly touched her cheek, then brushed his fingertips lightly against her throat—"you're driving me mad. Especially when you look at me like that."

Atalanta swallowed. "Like . . . what?"

"Like you want me to kiss you."

Atalanta opened her mouth to say yes—or no—or *something*—but no sound came out.

"Do you?"

"Do I?" she echoed, dazedly.

Stoke tilted her face up gently. Slowly he untied the ribbons beneath her chin and pushed her bonnet back, then cradled her face in his hands. His first kiss was soft, hardly a touch at all. The second was longer. By the third kiss, Atalanta had to grab on to the front of his coat to keep her balance. . . .

REGENCY ROMANCE
COMING IN DECEMBER 2005

Marry in Haste and *Francesca's Rake*
by Lynn Kerstan
Together for the first time, two Regency classics star
heroines gambling on love, not knowing if they will
lose their hearts—or win true love.

0-451-21717-9

Miss Clarkson's Classmate
by Sharon Sobel
Emily Clarkson arrives at her new teaching position
expecting her employer to be a gentleman, and she's
shocked to find a brute. He's expecting a somber old
maid. And neither is expecting the passion that soon
overtakes them both.

0-451-21718-7

Lady Emma's Dilemma
by Rhonda Woodward
Once lovers, Lady Emmaline and Baron Devreux have
different points of view concerning their long-ago
tryst. But in an unexpected encounter, the two simply
have too many questions and the answers only come
by moonlight—and with a little mischief.

0-451-21701-2

Available wherever books are sold or at penguin.com

My Lady Gamester

Cara King

A SIGNET BOOK

SIGNET
Published by New American Library, a division of
Penguin Group (USA) Inc., 375 Hudson Street,
New York, New York 10014, USA
Penguin Group (Canada), 90 Eglinton Avenue East, Suite 700, Toronto,
Ontario M4P 2Y3, Canada (a division of Pearson Penguin Canada Inc.)
Penguin Books Ltd., 80 Strand, London WC2R 0RL, England
Penguin Ireland, 25 St. Stephen's Green, Dublin 2,
Ireland (a division of Penguin Books Ltd.)
Penguin Group (Australia), 250 Camberwell Road, Camberwell, Victoria 3124,
Australia (a division of Pearson Australia Group Pty. Ltd.)
Penguin Books India Pvt. Ltd., 11 Community Centre, Panchsheel Park,
New Delhi - 110 017, India
Penguin Group (NZ), cnr Airborne and Rosedale Roads, Albany,
Auckland 1310, New Zealand (a division of Pearson New Zealand Ltd.)
Penguin Books (South Africa) (Pty.) Ltd., 24 Sturdee Avenue,
Rosebank, Johannesburg 2196, South Africa

Penguin Books Ltd., Registered Offices:
80 Strand, London WC2R 0RL, England

First published by Signet, an imprint of New American Library,
a division of Penguin Group (USA) Inc.

First Printing, November 2005
10 9 8 7 6 5 4 3 2 1

Printed in the United States of America

Chapter One

*R*ichard Stanton, tenth Earl of Stoke, strode up the cold marble stairs two at a time. Hundreds of candles in crystal chandeliers lit the mirrors on the walls around him and the red velvet between them, until the whole entrance hall glowed as if it were day.

What a waste. The beau monde certainly took their pleasures lavishly. And their duties lightly.

But he was one of them now, wasn't he? Stoke scowled at a powdered retainer who indicated the way to the drawing room.

Drawing room? Why didn't they speak plainly and call it the gaming room? He'd never seen a London townhouse look so much like a gaming club. Etched glass, burgundy damask—money to lure money.

Which was, presumably, the intention. The place smelled of money. Money, rich leather, candle smoke, and more money.

Stoke reached the high-arched entrance to the drawing room and he paused. He'd known that ladies gamed here— that was its attraction. But what he hadn't expected was their scent.

He'd been in enough gentlemen's clubs and gaming hells in his time to know the smell—but now that particular closed-in, thick smell was mixed with rose and lavender and delicate oils.

As he cast his gaze around the carved moldings and gilded cornices, the purr of cards being shuffled set his skin tingling. He swallowed. So this could still draw him?

The thought disturbed him more than he liked, but he pushed it aside. He was here to get Edmund. That was all.

A florid woman of middle age came up to him and held out both her powdered hands. "Lord Stoke! What a pleasure to see you here." Her voice was quick and animated. "You have never graced one of my little parties before, have you? Welcome. Do come and join the macao table. Or would you like some refreshment? We have a wonderful brandy."

That pulled his attention away from the crowd of gamesters around the central table. "Brandy?"

His disapproval must have shown, for she looked like a child caught teasing the cat. "Oh, it isn't smuggled, if that's what you think," she said, her voice playful. "Dear Bates had it left from before the war. *Do* stop scowling at me."

He'd never understand them. "I don't drink brandy." Realizing he sounded too curt, he added, "If you'd seen my men, Lady Isabella—"

"You're no longer in the army, Lord Stoke," she said with a pert smile. "Do sit down and enjoy yourself for once."

There was no point in arguing further. "Thank you," he said, glancing about the room. "Have you seen my younger brother anywhere?"

She gave him a knowing look. "He's at the macao table, I believe. He doesn't need rescuing, you know."

"Thank you," he said, sketching a bow.

He watched her as she strolled away. Like a spider in her web—except that she did not wish to eat the flies, just play with them. Gaming was a trap, and she might be as caught in it as the guests she drew to these gaming parties of hers.

Stoke strode over to the large table in the center of the

room. The green cloth on top was littered with cards and counters, and the occasional scribbled promise to pay. He quickly scanned the young men and women who surrounded the table, but Edmund was not there.

So where was the brat? Stoke had better things to do than play nursemaid to his baby brother.

Well, not *baby*. Edmund must be what—twenty now? Old enough to be past such starts. And old enough to resent being rescued from his favorite vice.

A cackling laugh called his attention to the corner of the room. There was Edmund's devil-may-care friend Ostenley, leaning over a two-person card table.

And there was Edmund. Playing cards with . . . oh hell, was that Malkham? What was Edmund doing playing with a shark like him?

Stoke approached the table. "Piquet?" he asked calmly.

Edmund turned quickly, his blue eyes resentful. Stoke was relieved to see his brother's gaze clear and sober beneath his carefully disordered brown curls. "Yes," the boy said challengingly.

"I thought you didn't like piquet."

Malkham looked up at this, his eyes sharp in his heavily lined face. "And good day to you, too, Stanton. Don't care to speak to me?"

Stoke's hand tensed on the back of his brother's chair. As he had done so many times in battle, he took a slow breath and gathered his emotions in a firm grip. "I beg your pardon, Lord Malkham," he said, his gaze steadily meeting the older man's. "I didn't notice you there. Good day."

Malkham rearranged the cards he held in a gnarled hand. "It's been a long time, Stanton. Oh, so sorry—it's Lord Stoke now, isn't it? Keep forgetting."

"That's quite understandable," he said, his tone easy. "You knew my father well, and it must feel strange to call me Lord Stoke instead of him."

"Knew him well," repeated the man, a cold smile on his dry lips. "Yes, indeed. Quite well."

The man always reminded him of a snake. And Edmund was gaming with him?

He turned his gaze on his brother's slightly flushed face. "I thought macao was your game."

Before Edmund could reply, Malkham set his cards face-down with a snap on the green baize table. "Macao is for children."

Macao was also harder to cheat at. "Most gamesters think otherwise," Stoke said, taking a look at the busy table in the center of the imposing room. "What's more daring than risking your money on luck alone?"

"Luck? Pshaw. Luck is for sniveling boys who want anyone to blame but themselves. Piquet is a game for men."

"And women?" said a new voice.

Stoke turned. He took one look at the tall woman standing there, and something he hadn't felt in years threatened to break through. Something . . . impulsive, perhaps.

He'd never seen a woman like her. Braids of shining hair the color of dark honey wound around her head, which she held high, as if in defiance. Her mouth was strong and resolute, but there was something in her green eyes—something cautious, almost scared.

And there was an energy, a resolve about her slender form that he recognized from his years in the battlefield. This was no schoolroom miss, no empty-headed butterfly. She wanted something, and was determined to get it.

As if she felt his gaze on her, her eyes glanced up to meet his. He felt a shock similar to recognition, but he knew he'd never seen her before tonight.

Her gaze flicked away immediately. She lifted her head even higher. "Do you dare play a woman, Lord Malkham?" she asked the wrinkled man, her voice low and rich.

"This is not a game for girls," was Malkham's reply.

"Are you afraid?" A ghost of a smile hovered about her lips, but her eyes were cold. "I heard you were a piquet player. I hoped for a game. Do you refuse me because I am female, or because I am an unknown to you?"

Malkham's lip twisted. "Don't know you from Adam. Or should I say . . . Eve?"

She raised her eyebrows serenely, as if she recognized his innuendo and considered it beneath her. "I am Miss Atalanta James, daughter to the late Viscount James," she said steadily. "You are Oswald, Lord Malkham. Now we have met. Will you play me, or no?"

The old man's eyes darted to Edmund and back to the girl. Deciding which was the richer pigeon to pluck?

"Well then," Malkham said with a sneer. "Let's see you play."

Beneath his hand Stoke felt Edmund tense. He pressed down warningly on the boy's shoulder.

Edmund tried to shake him off. "This is my game," he said, his voice tight.

"Come, come," said Malkham, with a narrow-eyed smile. "I concede, my dear boy. Keep your shillings."

Edmund stood so quickly his chair nearly overturned on the Persian rug. "I didn't expect such a lack of respect from you, sir," he said. "I had heard you were a serious card player. And you throw in our game to play a girl?"

Malkham reached into a coat pocket and withdrew a gold-inlaid snuffbox. "I *am* a serious player, boy." He flicked the lid open with one yellowing thumbnail. "But you are not. Discarding your queen, indeed."

"That's why it's called gambling."

"No, that's why it's called losing. Really now, it does not amuse me to play with children."

Edmund indicated the woman with contemptuous hand. "You're going to play with her."

"She may turn out to be a gamester, lad—something you are not."

Stoke placed a restraining hand on his brother's arm. "It's just as well your game is over, Edmund. India's colt is having trouble, and I wanted your help."

He locked gazes with his brother, and for a moment it was another war of wills. Then the boy relaxed. "Oh, very well. If you need me so desperately."

The mysterious woman stood just as straight as before. So she was really going to play Malkham? She must have no idea who the man was.

Unless she was an excellent player. Either way, it was not his business. He had enough to do to watch out for his brother and take care of his other duties. He could not be rescuing every green-eyed damsel who might or might not be in distress.

As if she knew his thoughts, her eyes glanced up to meet his. He had rarely seen such implacable resolve, and he wondered again what she was doing here. Her gaze dropped immediately, as if concealing something.

Whatever it was, it had nothing to do with him. "It has been a pleasure," he lied to Malkham and the mystery woman, sketching a bow. "Come, Edmund."

He could tell that Edmund had plenty to say, but luckily the boy kept his tongue until they reached the Ionic columns that flanked the ostentatious portico in front of the house.

Edmund turned to face him. "So tell me. Is India's colt having any trouble? Or was that just a ruse to fetch me home like a good boy?"

Stoke raised his eyebrows. "Would you rather have me announce in front of everyone that you're being sent home for being disobedient?"

Edmund slapped a plaster column in frustration. "I'm not a child."

"Then don't act like one."

"I was just having a game, that's all."

How many times had they gone over this same ground? "I told you before. I will no longer pay your gaming debts."

Edmund turned his sulky face away. "I don't see why not. You have heaps of money."

"You need to act like a man, Edmund. If I keep bailing you out, you will never learn."

"I know, I know," grumbled the boy. "When you were my age, you had been in the army for years, et cetera, et cetera, ad infinitum."

Stoke put his hand on his brother's shoulder and turned him to meet his gaze. "I am not going to argue with you. I will see you in debtor's prison before I pay another gaming debt." He wouldn't, of course, but he had to get through to the boy somehow. "If that is what it takes to teach you to think before you act, so be it."

Edmund looked uncertain for once. "I don't see why. All the fellows game. Cyril played hazard all the time, and you know father was always at the tables."

He held Edmund's gaze. "Gaming can be a fever. And I am not going to see you bankrupt our family by falling prey to it, whatever our brother or father did."

Edmund shrugged as much as his tight-fitting coat let him. "If you insist." He stared out into the dark street. "I daresay I should check on the colt anyway. Or were you intending to?"

Was he? As soon as he asked himself, he realized he had no intention of leaving yet.

The thought bothered him. It wasn't his duty to rescue a strange woman from the claws of Malkham. Nor was it his place. So why was he so determined to go back upstairs and protect her from the man?

As a captain in his regiment, he had taken care of his men. In the long year that he'd been the earl, he had assumed responsibility for his family, employees, retainers, tenants. What was one green-eyed miss to him?

Perhaps it was that sense of recognition he'd felt, that impulse that she was a kindred spirit. That might be what made him feel responsible for her. As if she were a—a younger sister, perhaps.

Edmund was staring at him. Stoke realized their coach had arrived, the red and white coat of arms painted on its side obvious even in this dim light.

Stoke cleared his throat. "No," he said slowly. "You take the carriage. There's something I need to do."

Atalanta felt her nerves tense as she took the chair opposite Lord Malkham. She'd never thought she'd be so easily distracted from her goal. She had everything planned and ready. So why did her mind keep straying to the dark-haired man who'd been here? She didn't even know who he was.

Maybe it was the way he looked after his younger brother. That touched something in her. How would it feel to be taken care of like that? To have someone you could depend on utterly?

She had no one but herself to take on the task before her.

Malkham. The name was ugly to her, unreal. Almost a legend, a story from her past. How strange, then, to finally meet him. Finally, after so many years of hating him.

She studied him, learning what she could from his face, his form. He wore his lank white hair long, after the fashion of his youth, so that it fell limply down to his hunched shoulders. The hands he rested on the cards were thin and gnarled, almost twisted, with large knuckles and cracked fingernails. His coat was modern, dark and restrained, but it hung loose on his frame in a way that implied a contempt for fashion.

But all this meant nothing when she looked into his face. It showed the man's soul—if it even existed. His skin was dull, heavily lined and pockmarked. His pale mouth was soft, almost slack, but his wrinkled eyelids hung low over eyes that were sharp enough to wound.

Sharp—and avaricious. There was no mercy in his face, no kindness, only dissipation and boredom.

That boredom was her way in. She schooled her features to reveal nothing—the gamester's face. "Standard rules, to a hundred points?"

"So," he said, his voice so low she could scarcely hear him. "*Are* you a gamester?"

She gave him the ghost of a smile. Let him wonder. "A crown a point?"

His beady eyes watched her in silence. What did he want? Was he trying to intimidate her?

She kept her jaw firm, returning his gaze steadily. Finally, he narrowed his eyes. "Miss *James,* did you say?"

She inclined her head. "I did."

"Daughter of the scholarly viscount, eh? Inherited his brains as well as his thirst for the cards?"

For a moment, she thought she was going to be sick.

She had to control herself. She had spent too many years waiting, learning, and planning to fail now.

She stiffened her resolve. "I enjoy a game or two," she said, fighting to keep all emotion out of her voice. She forced herself to take a slow, deep breath. "Shall we cut for deal?"

Chapter Two

Stoke waited until Edmund was safely off before heading back into Lady Isabella's utterly respectable version of a gaming hell.

It was ridiculous, of course, being here. How was he to rescue a lady to whom he'd never been introduced? And from the slimy clutches of a man she'd boldly sought out?

He made his way around damask-backed chairs and be-wigged footmen carrying refreshments until he reached the far side of the room, where the whist players sat over their cards in intense silence.

With his back safe against the wall, he surveyed the players. A good soldier knew the territory before striking. Whist, macao, piquet—he saw all the serious card games here. An open door led into the next room, where a group of older ladies gossiped and dealt.

So. Deep card games here, lighter ones in the other room. But no faro table, no dice for hazard—nothing to create a scandal or attract the law.

Just the lure to draw aristocratic wastrels in—privacy, comfort, and serious gaming. Lady Isabella offered all the pleasures of a gaming hell, coupled with the luxuries of a *ton* party. How could it fail to attract?

His hostess must have noticed that his hands were empty

of both drink and cards, for she approached him again. "Care to make a fourth at whist, Stoke? Or there's loo and speculation in the next room, if that's more to your taste."

In for a penny, in for a pound. "There's one thing you could do for me."

She gave him a knowing look. "Only one?" She dimpled at him. "No, I'm only quizzing you. What is it?"

His gaze moved back to the small table in the far corner. "Introduce me to Miss James?"

Lady Isabella turned to look. "Indeed. Miss Atalanta James, the Goddess of the Cards. So that's your taste?" She gave a wry laugh. "I can't fault you for it, though you'd have better luck at macao."

"Why is she called the Goddess of the Cards? Is she that good?"

His hostess looked amused. "She's good for a lady, certainly. But I fancy the gentlemen call her that because she is like a statue of a Greek goddess: beautiful and yet oh so cold to the touch. I have introduced many men to the goddess, but I've yet to see one win a smile from her."

He didn't care for the picture that painted. What were her relatives thinking, to permit such things? "I take it, then, that she games here regularly?"

"Recently, she does. Her great-aunt has a taste for loo. Come, I shall introduce you to the intriguing lady."

Lady Isabella moved gracefully between the tables, and he followed. "Her father was a noted gamester," she said. "Did you know that? Never knew a man with a greater love for the cards. It seems the viscount's fair daughter has inherited his passion."

They paused a few feet away from the piquet table. The girl looked so young sitting there, her back to him. Her crown of amber braids might be rigid, even flawless, but the long neck she held so straight seemed delicate and vulnerable.

She held her cards close to her chest, but he could see that she paused too long before taking a trick. She might think she was up to Malkham's level, but if she wasn't careful, she would end up just another of his victims.

Lady Isabella moved forward. "My dear Lord Malkham, what a charming partner you have tonight. Miss James—have you met the earl? He finds you quite fascinating, let me tell you."

Curse Lady Isabella. At her words, Miss James's eyes became guarded. Their hostess, as if satisfied with her mischief, gave a tinkling laugh and fluttered off to find new prey.

He had to remedy the situation. "Lady Isabella enjoys trying to discomfit me, as you see. Actually, Miss James, I was hoping for a game of piquet—when you and Malkham have finished. It is not often that one finds a lady with a flair for the game."

She paused for just a moment. "We have only just begun playing." Her voice was cool, revealing nothing.

"I should be pleased to wait on your convenience, if you are willing to play against me."

Malkham wrinkled his upper lip. "Stealing my partner, Stanton? Is this your new pastime or something?" His tone held just a hint of a sneer. "What, will no one else play with you?"

Stoke gave the old man a cold look. "I believe I asked the lady." He moved his gaze to the high-cheekboned face before him. "Will you do me the favor, Miss James?"

She inclined her head slightly. "It will be my pleasure."

That was clearly a lie. But as long as she played with him, he would have the chance to warn her off playing with sharpsters like Malkham.

He gave her a bow. "Until then."

As he turned away, he noticed that the hand she held her cards with was shaking slightly. Blazes take it all. What was it about her that made him feel so protective, so drawn to her? He had no room in his life for another charge. He already had trouble fulfilling all his duties.

So what in heaven's name was he doing?

Her luck was out tonight—not that she believed in luck. But here she was finally facing Lord Malkham across the piquet table, and this strange man showed up and asked her to game.

Of course she'd said yes. Whatever she did, she couldn't raise Malkham's suspicions. But why did it have to be tonight? She'd intended to play more than one game against Malkham, but now that their first game was drawing to a close she had no choice but to change opponents.

She fought to keep her hand steady as she picked up the last trick of the game. "Ninety-six," she said. Then she paused, as if the addition took her a second. "And . . . yes, I get ten for the cards, do I not?" She tried to sound cool but pleased. "I believe I win the game, Lord Malkham."

His eyes had a glint in them. "So you do, Miss James. My felicitations. And your winnings."

He pushed five golden guineas across the green baize table to her. She gave him her best girlish smile and scooped up the coins. "Would you like to play again sometime?"

"I would be honored." His dry lips smiled, but his eyes were as cold as ever. "I always enjoy a good partner," he said, his voice oily. "Particularly one as . . . pleasant to look at as you."

She wasn't certain she could keep her revulsion from showing, so she kept her eyes down as she put her winnings in her reticule.

She felt rather than heard the strange man appear behind her. Glancing up, she once again felt that odd sensation when she looked at his face. Those craggy brows, those intense, demanding eyes with their bronze glints—he looked like an untamed part of nature. Even his brown hair was streaked by the sun. What was a man like that doing in a place like this?

She did not know what he wanted with her, but she hoped she could sidestep it. She did not care to do battle with this man.

"My game, Miss James?" he said, his voice rich and deep.

She closed her reticule and stood regretfully. "I believe so."

The tall man put his hand beneath her elbow as if to lead her away. As if he owned her.

She turned back to Malkham. "Thank you for the game, my lord." She felt the hand beneath her elbow tense. Did the man's actions have to do with Malkham then, rather than her?

When in doubt, she thought, conduct yourself calmly and quietly, and let the fish hook itself. So she smiled to herself and let the forceful man lead her to a neighboring table.

As she sat in the crimson damask chair, she saw Malkham rise and leave the room. At least that was one difficulty out of the way—she needn't watch her every word, every step for a while. "Cut for deal?"

The earl eyed her for a moment, and she had to look away. It was ridiculous, but she felt like he could see into her soul.

But why should she care what he thought of her? She schooled her features into a polite mask and reached for the new pack of cards that a servant placed on the table.

He frowned at her for a moment, as if assessing her, then picked a card out of the stack. Before looking at it, he said, "Shilling points?"

Not a deep player, then. "Shilling points, to a hundred," she agreed. He turned over his card and she saw the queen of spades. She flipped up the seven of diamonds. "Your deal."

He frowned at the cards as he shuffled them. "Do you play much, Miss James?"

If he wanted information, he'd chosen the wrong partner. "On occasion."

"And do you enjoy it?"

"Enjoy it?" She tilted her head. "Do not most people enjoy cards?"

The pack of cards gave a crisp snap as he shuffled them. After a few seconds, he said, "I believe your father is deceased?"

His words hit her unaware. "I beg your pardon?" She could hear surprise and annoyance in her voice, and fought for tighter control.

He looked up, his expression changing to one of regret, almost embarrassment. "Forgive me, Miss James. I learned bluntness in the Peninsula, and in the year I have been back in England I have not managed to break myself of the habit. My servants threaten to leave because they say I treat them like raw recruits." She saw a glint of humor in his brown eyes. "Little do they know what I actually did to my new troopers."

He paused, tapping his fingers slowly against the table. "I mean only good to you, Miss James. I know I have no right to speak to you this way, but . . ." His fingers ceased their tapping. "Do you have someone to look out for you? A guardian, or older brother, perhaps?"

Why did he want to know? "I am properly supervised, I assure you."

He let out an exasperated breath. "I'm not trying to police you. But if no one has told you not to game with a sharp like Malkham, you need better advice." He picked up the pack of cards and began dealing.

She kept her gaze on the cards he dealt out. "Are you warning me he is dangerous? Is that it?"

He finished the deal and set down the remaining cards with a thump. "Yes, I am. You may think yourself a clever card player. Perhaps you are, in your way. But a man like Malkham—he lures you in, lets you win a little. Lays the groundwork. You become overconfident and the stakes go up, and that's when you realize you're no match for a—" He paused for a second, as if biting back the word he was about to say. "For a player of his experience," he finished wryly.

All her anger at his presumption flowed away in a moment, replaced by the awareness that this man was trying to protect her. He was blunt, and he thought he could order her around like one of his men, but that was inconsequential next to the warm feeling that enveloped her.

He cared. He hadn't even known her name, but he'd gone out of his way to warn her about Malkham. She wasn't used to that sort of attention, or concern.

She took a deep breath. "Thank you. I see you mean the best, and believe me—I am grateful." But how could she explain without revealing anything, or putting his back up? "I merely heard that Lord Malkham was a proficient card player. No one warned me not to game with him."

She studied her cards, and pulled a few out. "I discard four." She took four off the stack, noting that she still held no ace.

"I take the remaining four." He arranged his cards, then said, almost casually, "Will you promise me not to play Malkham again?"

This was too much. She gave him a steady look. "You have no right to ask me something like that."

He returned her gaze undeterred. "I know that. But will you promise me?"

She couldn't, of course. For all his annoying frankness,

she felt strangely touched by his request, but she couldn't grant it.

She looked down at her cards. "Point of five."

When he gave no response, she glanced up. He was still looking at her. Waiting.

But no matter what she thought of him, she had things to take care of. No one, not even someone as kind as him, would get in her way. "Point of five," she repeated.

"Stubborn, are you?" His voice contained grudging admiration. "Your point is good, by the way. So are you saying you intend to game with Malkham again? Why?"

He could try the patience of a saint. And she was no saint. "I declare a tierce," she said, pointedly looking at her cards.

"Are you that in love with cards? Could you not satisfy your yen with any other player?"

At the light in his eye, she felt her cheeks growing warm. This was not the time for feminine weakness. She must be strong. "I know you mean the best, Lord Stanton," she said. "And I am more grateful than you know. But I really cannot have you intruding into my private life."

He waved an arm at the glittering company around them. "This is private?" When she continued to stare stonily at him, he put his arm down and sighed. "I expect I was just rude again. Seems my lot in life. And I'm afraid Lady Isabella muddled our introduction, to boot. My family name is Stanton, yes, but my title is Stoke."

She felt dizzy for a second. That name . . . She swallowed convulsively. "I beg your pardon?"

"I was Captain Richard Stanton until a year ago, when I inherited the title—which, as a younger son, I had never expected—believe me. The outbreak of influenza last year took both my father and my elder brother. So almost overnight I went from cavalry officer to earl." He gave her a self-deprecating smile. "I am now Lord Stoke, for all my faults."

She closed her eyes. This could not be happening. Why?

What had she done to deserve this? "You are the Earl of Stoke?" Her voice sounded harsh in her ears.

"I am." His gaze was keen. "Does the name mean something to you? Did you know my father, perhaps?"

She fought for control. This meant nothing. Yes, he was a kind man—but that had no bearing on what she needed to do.

"No," she said finally. "I never met your father. Shall we play the game?"

His dark eyes held hers, and she felt as if they were struggling for control. She summoned up all her will, all her resolve, and looked down again at her cards. "Tierce?" she said again.

He paused, and she was afraid he would continue to press her. But he finally glanced down at his cards and said, "Good."

As they continued to declare their hands, her mind was in chaos. This changed everything. Though . . . perhaps it was all for the best. To find Stoke so easily was luck indeed.

Not that she believed in luck. Her father had taught her better than that.

At the thought of her father, she felt some of the tension leave her. She knew what she had to do. Nothing else mattered.

And she had Stoke right where she wanted him.

She soon realized he was a good card player. Part of her wanted to give the game her utmost effort, to see if she could best him—just for the challenge of it. But besting him in the long term meant restraining herself now.

She'd known from the moment she'd replaced her discards that he must hold four aces. That was child's play. But she declared her four kings boldly, confidently, as if she thought she could win with them. As if she were careless, or a novice player.

"Not good," he said, almost regretfully. She managed a slight look of surprise, looking down again at her cards as if she hadn't realized what he held. After a moment she gave a small "Oh" of dismay. Let him think she feared being capotted—that should finish the picture for him. Poor little Miss James, imagining herself a competent piquet player. How sad that she inherited her father's love for the cards without his skill.

She led out the king of hearts, which he took with his ace. He controlled the play for several tricks, but she finally got the lead back with the king of spades. Then she led out the rest of her hearts, in perfect order: queen, knave, nine, eight. Perfect order—the mark of a beginner.

She could see by his occasional hesitations that he was taking the bait, and believing her to be an unskilled player with simple, orderly habits. From his pauses she deduced he felt sorry to be winning money from an untutored player.

Let him. She would win all her losses back, and more. Much more. "So, you have ten for the cards," she said, as he took the last trick. "And—is it my deal?"

"Your deal," he agreed. He offered her a handful of cards.

When she took the cards from him, her fingers brushed against the back of his large, roughened hand. A hand that belonged to a real person, not an image in her mind, not a name—a man. A man who felt more comfortable on the battlefield than in high society, but who went out of his way to warn her when he thought she might be in danger.

A man she had sworn to bankrupt.

She stared at his hand, confused. After what his father had done to her family, she was perfectly in the right. But somehow she'd never thought of the new Earl of Stoke as a person.

"Would you rather I shuffle?" he said.

She took her hand away. "Please do."

With a deft touch, he gathered the cards together and began to shuffle them.

She had to fight this weakness. She had to think of her

sister, playing nursemaid for a bitter woman. And Tom, who would be lost without her.

And her father, who was gone. Forever. She was the only one left to take care of Tom and Louly, and she was determined to do it. Even if it took everything she had.

She took hold of her weakness, her girlish side, and shoved it down. The man across from her would be the first to say that in a war, the good are sometimes hurt. But if the end was just, then one did not shirk the fight. She might only be a girl of nineteen, but there was no one else to fight this battle.

She held out her hand for the cards. "My deal, I believe."

Chapter Three

*T*he waning afternoon sun slanted through the tall sash
windows of Stoke's office, illuminating the clouds of
dust particles floating in the air.

Stoke sneezed and reached for his handkerchief. This
was ridiculous. Had his father never used the office? The
amount of dust implied as much. As did the account books.

He wiped his nose, then reached for the pen. He'd never
expected to be writing his gaming debts into the ledger, but
fate loved springing surprises on him. He only owed the fair
Atalanta fifteen shillings, but he hadn't been able to pay it
the previous night.

Embarrassing, really. He hadn't intended to pay any
gaming debts of Edmund's, so he'd come to Lady Isabella's
empty-handed. And lost to Miss Atalanta James when the
lady had a streak of luck.

To be sure, he hadn't been playing his best. The scent of
her distracted him somehow. Yes, the Captain Stanton who
could advance unflinching into musket fire and artillery
charges had somehow become Lord Stoke, distracted at
cards by a hint of violet.

So although he had meant to show her she wasn't as good
a player as she thought, he had ended up owing her fifteen

shillings, despite her tendency to leave her kings unprotected.

Stoke wrote the entry in the account book and wiped his pen. He would need to call on her to pay her the money. The thought disturbed him, and he did not care to be disturbed. She might be slender and graceful, with delicate hands and soft skin, but he had known beautiful women before. He should not be so affected.

The clatter of top boots in the hall told him Edmund was back from his ride. Five seconds later, the office door opened with its customary squeak.

At the sight of Edmund's flushed face, Stoke set down his pen and began to rise. "Is one of the horses ill?"

Edmund threw his crop down on a brown leather chair. "How could you?"

Stoke observed the boy's mulish countenance and sat back down in his chair. "If you have something to say, then say it. How could I what?"

"Oh, as if you don't know." Edmund marched forward and leaned on the desk, staring across it at Stoke. "So I am not supposed to game, am I? Oh no, no wagers for Edmund, no cards for Edmund, heaven forbid Edmund should go to a racecourse or prize fight! But you? Oh, you can game. You're the earl. You inherited all the money, so you can do whatever you please."

"Enough." His tone brooked no debate. "You have a generous allowance, but you prefer to lose it all on hazard or macao within days of receiving it. And you question my decision?"

"It looks rather one-sided from where I'm standing."

"Then take a look from my side." Stoke shoved the ledger across the desk to him. "There you have it. So far this year, I have lost fifteen shillings at cards, and nothing from wagering on dice, horses, or boxing. And you call me unjust?"

Edmund flopped down into the padded armchair behind him. "Well, it's not right to blame me for my losses. My luck was out. Had you let me continue, I know I could have recouped all my losses, and more. I could feel it."

He knew that line of thought. Too well. "Don't listen to that feeling," he said. "It lies. No matter how much your gut tells you it's a matter of luck, your head should tell you it's no such thing. It's random chance, and you know it."

Edmund threw his hands up in frustration. "I thought you understood, Richard. You have felt it, haven't you? When you have the dicebox in your hand, and your whole body knows what the roll will be? Tell me you don't know what I mean."

He had no idea how to reach his brother. "I know what you mean," he told him. "But that feeling signifies nothing. Believe me. Our father believed in the goddess of luck, as did Cyril. And take a look at what they did to the estate."

"It's not so bad."

"It is in chaos. There are many things father could have done to further our family's standing. Instead, he played faro. He played hazard. He played anything and everything, as long as it involved wagering. By God, he even had packs of playing cards printed up with the family coat of arms on the backs! That was his great ambition for the family, Edmund—the red griffins that our ancestors carried proudly into battle became nothing more than whimsical decorations on the backs of cards that were meant to be used once, then thrown away."

Edmund gave a guilty grin. "Think we still have a few of those packs lying about the place. Always did like them, when I was a boy. Why play with a pack that has ordinary plain white backs, when you can have griffins? That's what I thought."

"But think of the expense just to print the cards, not to mention how much father and Cyril lost with them."

"They didn't do that badly."

Stoke shook his head. "Granted, their losses did not much exceed their winnings, so our finances are in tolerable shape. But the estate? Father's improvements were sporadic, and rarely recorded. Debts, monies owed us, contracts—I don't think he wrote many of them down. The records are a shambles."

Edmund shrugged. "Poor you, having so much money you have to spend all your time writing it in little columns."

Stoke slapped his hand down on the desk. "I didn't ask for this." He took a deep breath, letting his anger ebb. "I didn't ask for this," he repeated more quietly. "My life is my regiment."

"You mean *was*."

It took a brother to see all your weaknesses. "Yes, *was*. This is my life now. I was not raised to it, but I am doing my best to fulfill my duties."

"But I'm not you."

Stoke rubbed futilely at his temples. How could he make his brother see what was so obvious to him? He cast his mind back to the reasons why he cared so much. "We're part of a line, Edmund," he said, struggling to put his thoughts into words. "Part of a family. What we do reflects on the name of Stoke, just as our ancestors' actions reflect on us."

Stoke rose and strode over to a glass-fronted bookcase. "Let me show you." He pulled out a tall volume, its soft leather cover embedded with centuries of dust.

He put the book on the desk and gingerly leafed through the musty pages. "Here," he said, pointing to a page covered with tiny sums in faded blue ink. "John Stanton, third Earl of Stoke. This is his accounting."

His eyes alight with curiosity, Edmund jumped out of his chair and crossed to the desk. "I never knew we had things like this." He bent down to read the writing. "Not a very good speller, was he?"

Stoke relaxed into a grin. "Not much of a breeder, either, if his repeated expenses for amorous phylacteries are what I think they are. He never did have any children, and his nephew Edmund Stanton became the fourth earl."

"Really?" Edmund turned the page. "I never learned any of this. Was I named for him?"

"Indirectly. He was killed fighting for Charles the First at twenty-two."

Edmund made a face. "What a waste."

"Perhaps. But he fought for his country, for what he believed in. And when the next Charles came to the throne, Edmund's son was well rewarded."

Stoke closed the book carefully. "There are more of them," he said. "A Stanton died defending Stoke in the time of King Stephen. He died, but his name, his family, his vassals lived on. Do you see why I feel as I do?"

Stoke could recognize that his brother was impressed, though trying not to show it. "I suppose," Edmund said carelessly. Then, as if remembering his original grievance, he scowled. "But I still don't see what's so different about you gaming with Atalanta James." Edmund crossed his arms across his chest. "Or do your rules not count when you have a woman in your sights?"

That wasn't what he was doing, was it? Pursuing the girl? He waved a dismissive hand. "What I do is not your concern."

"So I must stop playing to preserve the sacred name of Stanton, but you—no, for you things are different."

Edmund dropped down loosely into the armchair. With a sigh, he brushed back his curly hair. "You used to be a younger brother yourself," he said resentfully. "I thought you might understand. Idiotic, wasn't it? Now that you're the earl, you're above the rest of us. Do as I say, not as I do, right?"

Stoke had made a mess of it this time. If he was to win

his brother over, he had to come clean. "I wasn't playing deep," he said, leaning across the desk to emphasize his words. "And I wouldn't have played at all, except I don't like to see innocents plucked by Malkham."

"Oh, you were gaming with her to protect her?" Edmund sounded cynical.

"Perhaps I found her . . . intriguing. That may have affected my decision, I admit it. But I do not play deep." He paused, knowing that Edmund would never accept such a superficial explanation.

It went against the grain with him to confide in anyone, but he had never shirked his duty, and this was not time to begin. "I saw what gaming did to Cyril," he said reluctantly. "And how it absorbed our father. Before I entered the army, I think I felt the same . . . lure. But I will not give in to it any more than I intend for you to."

Edmund looked slightly mollified. "If you were really trying to save Atalanta James, you may as well throw in the towel. She isn't called Goddess of the Cards for nothing."

He felt his muscles tense. "Is she an inveterate gamester?"

"Not half," Edmund said admiringly. "Her father ruined himself at the card table, did you know? Looks like she's primed to follow him. Not that she has much inheritance to lose."

Nothing made sense concerning the mysterious Atalanta. "If she has so little, who is paying for her season in London?"

Edmund grinned. "She won it off her cousin at the table—that's what Ostenley says. Got to admire her nerve, I say."

He'd never heard the like. "She won her season in a card game? I wonder what she'd have paid if she lost."

Edmund's grin became decidedly wicked. "Do you think

she'd play me? I could think of ways for her to pay me what she owed."

He restrained the urge to plant his little brother a facer. "If you touch her," he said clearly, "you won't live to see what hit you."

Edmund flushed. "I was only joking. I'm no Captain Sharp, extorting women's favors."

"No. Of course you aren't," he said awkwardly. Why was he so touchy over the girl?

"See here, Richard—if you do mean to stay away from the gaming table, then stay away from Atalanta James. You may be able to protect her from Malkham, but you cannot protect her from herself."

The truth of that cut deep, but he was not one to give up easily. "She is young yet," he argued, unsure who he was trying to convince. "Perhaps she can yet be cured."

"By you?"

That was the crux of the matter. "I don't understand it myself." He stared down at the tan leather of the account book. He had already gamed once for her, and she hadn't even asked him to. In trying to save her, might he end up lost himself? He didn't have the right to take chances like that— not now that he was the earl.

But why was it that his duty was always at odds with whatever he wanted most? He shook his head. "I need to call on her to pay her what she won. I do not expect to see her more after that."

Edmund leaned back in his chair. "So, one last time?"

"Yes."

Edmund grinned wickedly. "Funny. Every time I sit down at the gaming table, that's just what I tell myself."

"Someone to see you, miss."

Atalanta felt her heart leap in her chest, and told it to behave. This was ridiculous. Of course it wasn't the Earl of Stoke—and if it was, she didn't care one whit.

She covered up the papers she had been studying at the paltry desk that her cousin allowed her to keep in her bedroom. "Thank you, Maggie," she said. "Do you know who it is?"

The maid gave her an airy look that meant she knew who was in charge in this household, and it wasn't Atalanta. "Couldn't say, miss. Some fellow."

"Thank you. That will be all."

The maid sauntered off and shut the door with a loud thump behind her.

Atalanta frowned at the white panels of the door. She did not enjoy being the poor relation. She did not enjoy seeing the servants smirk at her, or bearing the cold shoulder Cousin Harriet invariably showed her. So if this was Lord Stoke, then he was a welcome change, a dash of color in her dark life in London.

In spite of his name.

Atalanta strode over to the dull pier glass and checked her hair and gown. Her practical braids were still neat, and her gown might pass muster, if Stoke did not look too closely.

Squelching a sudden wish to appear more fetching, she made her way down to the wood-paneled upper hall of her cousin's aging townhouse. The door to the drawing room was open, and she headed that way.

"Psst!"

No, it couldn't be. But when she glanced around, there was her scapegrace stepbrother hiding behind a large vase. He might have reached the lofty age of sixteen, but he always seemed more boy than man to her. Especially when crouching behind vases.

"Psst!" he hissed, waving frantically at her.

So it wasn't Stoke after all. "Tom," she whispered, peering behind the green porcelain vase, "what are you doing there?" Her worry over him helped distract her from an embarrassing feeling of disappointment that he wasn't the earl. "Now that I think of it," she said, "what are you doing in London at all? I know Eton isn't on vacation right now."

He looked around furtively, his shaggy brown hair falling into his eyes. "Is there somewhere we can talk?"

"What's wrong with the drawing room?"

"Your relatives are in there. So when the maid left, I decided to stay here," he whispered, brushing his hair back with an impatient hand. "Your relatives don't like me."

"Can't think why." At his beseeching smile, she softened. "Very well. I'll fetch my bonnet, and we can go for a walk. But whatever you do, don't break the vase while I'm gone."

"Can I do it when you get back?"

She glared, and he pretended to cower. With a shake of her head, she strode up the thinly carpeted stairs to her room. What in the world was she going to do with him?

It took just a moment for her to fix a pale blue bonnet over her braids and grab her treasured blue velvet pelisse, and head back down the stairs. Tom was where she had left him, and he followed her as quietly as his sixteen-year-old feet could manage.

Atalanta pulled on her pelisse as she stepped out into the fresh air. She took a deep breath and savored it. She was tired of too many late nights, too many tonnish card rooms smoky from too many candles. Though London air smelled too murky, too close to be mistaken for country air, it was better than a stale drawing room.

Fastening her pelisse, she gazed at the rows of tall white townhouses which blocked most of the sky. What little they didn't block was covered with dark gray clouds.

No, she realized, there was a bit of blue to the north. "This way," she told Tom, setting out toward the glimpse of sky. "Now out with it. What are you doing away from school?"

He stuck his hands in his pockets, looking very much a schoolboy. "Took a holiday."

Had she been that young at sixteen? She didn't think so. Her father's death had changed her years before. "Tom," she said, striding energetically up the street, "if you don't tell me right now, you will face the wrath of Atalanta James. And you know you don't want to do that."

That brought a grin to his face, just as she'd hoped it would. "Right, then. The truth. I might have been sent down."

That brought her to a halt. "Sent down? Tell me you're not serious."

He gave her a half-cocky, half-shameful grin. "Wasn't my fault, entirely. Old Beak-Face wanted me to sneak on someone. And telling tales is beneath Tom James. Or Tom Vanley. Or whatever my name is this week."

She hooked her elbow through his. "You're a James," she told him, resuming her pursuit of the lone patch of blue. "You may not have James blood, but my father wanted you to have his name. And I'm proud to call you brother."

"I daresay I shall remain a James then, as my mother is too busy with Weasel-Breath to come back to England and call me son."

Tom pulled away from her arm, took a running jump upward, and tried to touch the crossbar of the black iron lamppost they were passing.

"Belay that," he said, jogging back to her. "Tom James does not ask for any man's pity. Or any sister's. My mother can live with Weasel-Breath if she likes. I have you. You're prettier anyway."

She took his arm again and gave it a squeeze. "Some people are just weak, Tom. Your mother didn't want to be poor."

He rolled his eyes. "I know, I know, you've told me a thousand times. It wasn't me, it was the money."

"Sometimes I think it's always the money." She gazed at the Corinthian pillars of the house they were passing. "People do disturbing things for money."

"Speaking of which," he said with a grin, "Percy and I have a grand scheme. We're going to be rolling in wealth in no time."

Thus spoke a boy with no common sense. "Don't tell me. You've started a faro bank at Eton, and that's why you were sent down?"

He chuckled. "You have good ideas, sis. Wish that were the reason. No, I got booted out because old Beak-Face saw someone climbing out my window in the middle of the night."

"And he thought it was you?"

Tom pulled away and made another flying leap at a lamppost. "Nope—he could see that much. What he wanted was the name of the fellow, and when I wouldn't supply it— well, you can guess the rest."

"Oh, Tom." She couldn't reproach him, not really. "But why did you let the other boy climb out your window?"

"My window leads to a tree that hangs over the outside wall—all the fellows use it when they want to escape the tortures of the old prison. Wouldn't be right to say no."

"Not right?" She shook her head. "I'll never understand schoolboy ethics. Why were the boys sneaking out, anyway? To go drinking?"

"Something like that."

Seeing his roguish expression, she groaned. "Boys. I should have known. And you're the one who got sent down."

"Beak-Face has been looking for an excuse to kick me out for years. Finally got his little beak-faced wish."

Atalanta walked on in silence for half a block, staring regretfully at the procession of gleaming brass door-knockers that announced the wealth and security of the inhabitants.

She might not be able to give her siblings wealth, but she would do anything to give them the security they deserved, the security she'd once taken for granted, before she'd lost it so suddenly and completely. "How much will that commission cost?" she asked. "The one Percy's brother can arrange?"

Tom turned an excited face to her. "I can have it for just four hundred pounds. Do you mean you have the funds?"

"Four hundred pounds?" That was the bargain he'd been boasting of? She'd had no idea an ensigncy cost so much. "I'm sorry, Tom. I don't have it yet."

He tried to hide his disappointment, but his face was so expressive she always knew what he was thinking. "The card thing didn't work?" he asked casually.

"It's going to take time." But it looked like she no longer had the luxury of time.

She stared fiercely at yet another brass knocker. "No," she finally said, "I'll manage somehow. I will. Don't worry about it."

He jumped up onto an ornate iron railing and tried to balance between the spiky finials. "Can I help?"

"Don't do that—" She started toward him, but he jumped down before she could grab him, tearing the hem of his dusty brown coat.

"I'm bunking with a friend of Percy's in Covent Garden, so I'll be in town to do any spy work you want done." He grinned. "I know how to pick pockets and pick locks, too."

"No thank you, very much!" She tried to wipe the dust off the back of his coat, but he was too quick for her.

"Let me do something! I can help. I may not be the head of the family, but I'm a deal smarter than that oatmeal-eating viscount you call cousin."

That was all she needed—Tom spying through keyholes

and picking Lord Malkham's pocket. "Just take care of yourself," she said, wishing she could straighten his rambunctious hair. "Don't do anything criminal for a day or two, please? I may be able to raise the money sooner than planned."

Tom shrugged, stretching the seams of his dusty coat. "No, don't worry about it, sis. I won't need your money." He took a run at the next lamppost, and this time managed to jump high enough to grab the crossbar.

Hanging in the air, his coat straining at the seams, he gave her a gleeful grin. "Percy and I have found the most ripping scheme," he called down to her. "I'll be pouring the gold into your lap any day now."

She didn't like the sound of this. "What sort of scheme is it?"

Tom kicked his legs forward and started to swing back and forth. "Percy knows a fellow who has an inside lead to some copper mines in Peru. He'll let us in on the money, as long as we each bring five more investors into the project. And the best part is—we get to keep a commission on each investor we find, and on each of the investors they bring, and so on!"

Her stepbrother had never possessed an ounce of common sense, but this? How could he fall for a thing like this? "Tom, you know it will never work!" she called up to him. "Where will you get five investors? And what do you know about copper mining in Peru?"

Tom's hands slipped off the iron bar, and he crashed to the pavement. "That's the beauty of it, Atalanta," he said, staggering up and rubbing his backside. "I don't have to know anything. I just buy in, and I'm a made man."

How could he not see what was so obvious to her? "Didn't my father teach you how to spot this sort of rat? And at a hundred paces? Tom, anything that claims to be a short-cut to riches has a catch, at the very least. At the worst, it's some sort of swindle. Besides, where will you get the money to buy in?"

Tom gave a careless shrug. "Percy can lend me the rhino. Look, I know it's a risk, but what else is there for me? I've never been friendly with books, and you know it's only Lady Luck who's kept me from being sent down before now. Don't worry about me, sis. I can take care of myself."

He looked so young as he said it. So unsure of himself. And he was clearly not capable of taking care of a canary, let alone himself.

She had to get that money for his commission. And soon. The army was the only place she could think of where his energy would be put to good use. With any luck, marching several miles a day would cure him of foolish stunts like leaping at lampposts.

The problem was, if she didn't get the money soon it would be too late. Even if she talked him out of this scheme, he was certain to find another one around the corner.

"Don't rush into anything, Tom," she said, trying to sound lighthearted. "I've figured out a way to hurry my gaming plan."

"Really?" His eyes lit up. But almost instantly, he glanced down and looked embarrassed. "No, don't bother yourself, sis. I'm not even your brother, really. If you get any money, it can be your dowry. I'd love to see you married off to a fat old parson, with a passel of squalling kids to dote on."

"So I only rate a fat old parson? Thank you kindly."

He grinned. "And I wager he'll be bald, too. Or if you don't want your parson, then save the money for Louly. God knows she must be frog-faced living at Cousin Harriet's, wiping the noses of those little monster children."

His words gave her a pang. Even more than Tom, her failure to protect Louly gnawed at her. "I'm going to rescue her, Tom." She squared her shoulders and stiffened her resolve. "I will. And I'll get you your commission too, see if I don't."

The spot of blue had vanished from the sky, but Atalanta marched on with renewed vigor. "Father might not have been able to provide for the three of us, but I will. And I won't let anything get in my way."

In her mind, she saw the face of Lord Stoke. "Or anyone." She might not like it, but she knew she had to do whatever she could, no matter the consequences—to her or to anyone else.

She crossed her arms over her chest and smiled grimly at her stepbrother. "So, what do you say, Tom?"

He must have heard something new in her voice, for he turned and actually looked at her. "What do I say to what?" As the realization hit him, his eyes grew wide. "You don't mean—"

"Yes, I do." There was no turning back now. "Do you still want to be my spy?"

Chapter Four

*L*ord Stoke stood on the doorstep, in the wind, waiting for the footman to size him up.

This was not something that usually happened to the Earl of Stoke. Nor had it happened to Richard Stanton since his promotion to lieutenant years ago.

He raised his eyebrows with all the hauteur of a long line of Stokes. "I wish to see Miss James," he repeated. But the lanky young footman only scratched at his curly black hair. "Miss Atalanta James. Now."

He barked out that last word as he would a command to a green trooper. The footman started, then ducked his head. "Please come in, sir," he stammered. "I will get the lady."

He'd never seen such an inexperienced footman. "Take my coat first, lad." He thrust his greatcoat into the hands of the staring young man. "Next, show me to the drawing room. Lastly, send word to your young mistress."

"To . . . my young mistress?" His mouth gaped open, and he looked in danger of dropping the greatcoat.

"Miss James."

"Oh." The young man jerked in what must be an attempt at a bow. "Yes, sir. Right away."

The black-haired lad bustled away with the coat, then hurried back. "This way, sir."

As Stoke strode up the stairs after the boy, he studied the inside of the narrow townhouse. A patched rug here, a stain on the wallpaper there—it all added up to a severe shortage of funds.

Genteel poor, were they? Was that why they could afford no better servants?

The footman showed him into the drawing room nervously. "This is Lord, uh . . ."

He was hopeless. "Stoke."

"Lord Stoke, ma'am. To see Miss Atalanta." The footman gave another jerky bow, and scurried out of the faded but elegant room.

The sharp-faced woman sitting on the brown brocade sofa looked up, but she did not rise or even nod her head. This must be the relative with whom Atalanta James was staying in London.

"Lord Stoke?" Her voice was thin and tight, and her gray eyes watched him closely from beneath a tight crown of dun-colored curls. "Here to see my cousin? Do you know her?"

He didn't know how the lady would react to hearing he was here to pay a gaming debt, so he gave her a slightly bored smile. "I met Miss James at a rout recently. The late Viscount James was a friend of my father's, so I thought I should pay a courtesy call."

"Indeed." She still watched him through her pale eyes, and she did not invite him to sit down. "I take it you met her at Lady Isabella's?"

That could be a bad sign. Did this cousin disapprove of Lady Isabella? Or, more likely, of her gaming parties?

Unfortunately, he had no other answer for her. "Yes, I did meet Miss James at Lady Isabella's. I take it you are Mrs. Norris?" Always one to scout out the territory ahead of time, he had acquainted himself with the names of Atalanta's relatives against just such an occasion.

"I am." Her scratchy voice was as cold as her eyes. "I take it your father was Stoke the gamester?"

She made it sound like Ivan the Terrible. "My father was partial to cards, yes." He strolled over to the tall sash windows and glanced out at his horses. Peter had their heads, and they looked calm.

"Tell me, Lord Stoke—do you share your father's passion for gaming?"

Either the lady took exception to his father, or to gaming in general. Not that there was much difference between the two. "It depends on my mood," he said calmly, hoping to turn the subject. If Mrs. Norris hated cards, he would do Atalanta James no good by seeming to be a gambling associate. "Are you enjoying town, Mrs. Norris?"

"As much as we are able." Her smile was thin.

"I see." He was thinking of uttering some platitude about the prospect from the window when he smelled the delicate scent of violets.

He turned, and for a moment he thought Atalanta looked like a flower herself. Her high-necked gown was a delicate shade of blue which contrasted strikingly with her dark golden braids. And her eyes—he'd never seen green eyes so alive.

She didn't see him for a moment, but entered the drawing room with a graceful walk. She gave her cousin a polite smile, then she turned her face toward him, as if feeling his presence as he felt hers.

"Miss James," he said, with a formal bow. "You may not remember me. I am Richard Stanton, Earl of Stoke. We met recently at Lady Isabella's." There. That should scotch any fear that he was Miss James's dedicated gaming companion.

He could tell Atalanta caught his meaning immediately. "Lord Stoke. Of course," she said, in a voice that said she didn't remember him at all. "How kind of you to call. I take it you have met my cousin?"

He smiled at her. "Yes, I have."

"Certainly," said the pale-eyed Mrs. Norris in her reedy voice. "This Stoke is one of your friends from the gaming table, is he not? He says your fathers were friends."

Atalanta looked startled for a moment, before her customary calm settled over her. "I believe they knew each other, yes," she said, not meeting his gaze. "I believe my father once . . . mentioned the previous Lord Stoke."

The older lady gave Atalanta a hard smile. "I'm sure he did. And now here you are, fast friends with the son. Like father, like daughter, eh?"

Atalanta drew herself up proudly, but Stoke could see her hands trembling. "If I in any way resemble my father," she said in a low voice, "I take pride in the fact. He was a noble man."

"Of course." The cousin had a sour expression. "As you never tire of telling us."

He could see Atalanta's nostrils flare, and for a second he thought she was going to say something cutting. Instead, she turned on her heel and marched out of the drawing room, her head held high.

He turned to her acidic cousin. "Thank you for your hospitality, ma'am." He gave her a bland smile, as if nothing untoward had been said. "Good day."

He followed Atalanta out the door, hoping she hadn't escaped him.

Now then. What was he doing chasing her? He had merely come to pay his debt—that was all. He couldn't rescue her, even if that dragon of a cousin begged to be slain.

But he had escaped from the life she followed now. He had learned truer happiness in his regiment, on a horse, and even managing his estates than he'd ever found at the green baize table.

If he could escape, couldn't she? Perhaps she just needed

a nudge in the right direction. And if her cousin exemplified her family, she had no one in her life to give her that nudge.

He emerged from the stuffy drawing room and glanced about. There she was, ascending the narrow staircase with her blue skirts flowing about her.

This was the time for speed, not subtlety. "Miss James," he called up the stairs. "You forgot that drive in the Park you promised me."

She stopped, one foot on the landing. She stood unmoving for a moment, then turned her head until he could see her delicate profile. "I beg your pardon?"

He strode to the bottom of the steps. "This is a perfect day for a drive. The sky is blue, the air is warm—how can you say no?"

Her hand on the bannister, she pivoted to face him. "How?" Her voice held a challenging note, and he could see the fire still in her eyes.

He grinned up at her. "Very well, I lied. It's cold, and there isn't an inch of blue sky to be found—but at least it isn't raining. What do you say?"

She looked away, but not quickly enough to hide her smile. "I don't know if that would be wise."

"Of course it's wise. And if you're a good girl and don't spook the horses, I'll play piquet with you the next time we meet."

That got her attention. By God, she was mired in deep.

After a moment she smiled at him, but her eyes held little warmth. "I accept your offer," she said, her voice brisk. "Are your horses outside?"

They were, though he had not planned to take her driving when he came here. Atalanta James had a way of oversetting all his plans. "All is ready, Miss James," he assured her.

"I'll be down in one minute."

He'd heard that before, but the wonder was, she was

telling the truth. Less than a minute later she descended the staircase, still fastening a snug blue velvet pelisse.

He looked at her flushed face with pleasure. "Do you need to tell your cousin you're going out?"

"No." Her tone was matter-of-fact, but her eyes were guarded.

She led the way down to the front door, and he had to move quickly to open it before she did. Did the servants do nothing in this house, that she was so accustomed to hauling the door open herself?

Or did they only do nothing for Miss Atalanta James?

She gave him a little smile as he held the door for her, but for once the smile reached her eyes. It was sad, really, that the small act of someone opening a door for her could please her so.

She stepped lightly down the few steps to the flagstones and stopped abruptly. "Oh my goodness," she said, sounding breathless. "What beauties!"

She headed straight for his jet-black carriage horses. "How splendid!" She nodded to the groom who held their heads, his red-and-white livery rather splendid itself despite the gloomy day.

Atalanta stood in front of the horses for a moment, letting them see her, then reached out and stroked their noses. "And such elegant heads."

She stepped to the side and began examining the beasts as closely as if she were thinking of buying them. "What necks!" She stroked the neck of the nearer horse with a firm hand. "And such a perfectly matched pair. Even their legs—oh, look at their hocks. Do they have the same dam?"

What a change had come over her. This girl was nothing like the collected creature at the card table. And she clearly knew horses. "Yes, they do," he said. "You have a good eye."

She smiled up at him, her whole face lighting up. "I adore

your horses. Do they go well together? What are their names?"

She was delightful standing here, fresh and animated in the warm glow of sunlight. "The one you're currently admiring is Lucifer, and the far one is Rogue."

"Nonsense," she said warmly, stroking the black horse's cheek. "They're darlings, absolute darlings. Lucifer, indeed!"

He grinned at her indignation. "You've fallen for their innocent act. If you saw Rogue nipping at Lucifer's flank when they're being harnessed, you might see things differently."

"Of course I wouldn't." She circled around to Rogue and patted his neck. "That's nothing but high spirits. And you are high-spirited, aren't you, my handsome? And doesn't Lucifer kick you sometimes when no one's looking?"

"He'd better not."

She grinned over the horse's back at him. "Did you breed them?"

He patted Lucifer, glad to see his coat was pristine as always. "I'd love to say I did, but that distinction belongs to a friend of mine. But since I've been back in England, I have been doing a bit of breeding."

"Oh, tell me about it," she said, her eyes glowing.

He indicated the waiting curricle. "Why don't we discuss it while driving through Hyde Park?"

She gave a wry grin. "Getting carried away, was I? It's just been so long."

She climbed into the carriage without waiting for a helping hand, and settled herself confidently on the driver's side. He was going to protest when he saw her laughing eyes.

"Do move over, there's a good girl," he said.

She dimpled at him. "Only if you promise to let me drive later."

He paused, his foot on the step. "My team have very delicate mouths."

"So do I, so I know how they feel." Her grin was decidedly mischievous. "No, really, I'm an excellent whip. My father made certain of that. And if I so much as make Lucifer twitch an ear, you can take back the reins. Agreed?"

Something tightened in his chest. She was a danger to him—he'd known it from the start. But how cowardly to run from a little danger.

He looked up into her misty green eyes and felt like he could lose himself in them, and be a happier man for it. "Agreed," he finally said.

She smiled gleefully and slid over to the passenger side. "You'll see—I never land my passengers in the briars."

"I feel so much calmer now, Miss James." He climbed the rest of the way into his well-balanced curricle and adjusted the reins. "Are you seated comfortably?"

"Indeed," she said. "Do give them their head—they must be moped from standing still so long."

He nodded to Peter, who released the horses and scampered around to climb up behind. Then with a gentle motion of the reins, Stoke alerted his team. They went up into their collars, and at a word from him they stepped forward.

"Oh, I knew it," she said. "They're treasures. Do you ever race with them?"

"Once or twice, but not recently." He'd been too busy with the estate to indulge his usual pleasures.

Now why was that? Surely he could find the time.

He eased his horses down the street and toward the Park. "I take it your family breeds horses?"

She looked about her with evident pleasure. "We used to. Did you ever hear of the James stables? We didn't have too many carriage horses—that wasn't my father's forte—but our hunters were prized."

"Oh, of course." He should have seen the connection immediately. "Is all your family horse-mad?"

She chuckled—a warm, easy sound. "My cousin Harriet's branch of the family never had the taste for it, but my father raised all of us in the stables, more or less."

He took a moment to negotiate the crowded turn at Hyde Park Corner, easily skirting a rickety landau drawn by equally rickety horses. "And who are 'all of us'? You have siblings, I take it?"

She twisted around to examine a high-stepping mount behind them. "Don't like those feet," she said. "Idiot. Oh, sorry. I didn't mean to change the subject."

She settled back against the well-sprung seat. "Yes, my siblings are indeed horse-mad, as you call it. Tom was a dab hand at training shy horses to jump, and Louly—well, she was really too young to do anything but sit on a horse back when our father died."

She paused. When there was a break in the traffic, he glanced over to see if he had trod on dangerous ground.

She looked sober, but not in distress. Perhaps if he drew the conversation back to his horses, it would be easier for her.

Past the commotion of Hyde Park Corner, the beginning of Rotten Row was relatively empty. "Would you like to take the ribbons?" he asked, hoping to bring her smile back.

It worked. She sat up straight and moved slightly toward him so she could hold the reins evenly. "Yes, please," she said demurely.

Atalanta James might be unpredictable and contradictory, but one thing she was not was demure. "Now behave yourself."

She wrinkled her nose at him. "You're an older brother, aren't you? Well, I'm the oldest, too, and I'm not accustomed to being ordered about, I give you fair warning."

"I'll keep it in mind."

She took the reins with a light but firm hand. So far, so good.

Perhaps she noticed his tenseness. "I do know how to drive."

She never gave up. "You just finished telling me you bred hunters, not carriage horses."

"Don't put words in my mouth."

But it seemed all his worrying was for nothing. She was surer with the horses than she was at cards, and she didn't make nearly as many mistakes.

When the parade of carriages and riders grew denser, she slowed the team in a way that kept them calm. "I expect you and I quarrel so much," she said, "because we're both eldest children and accustomed to telling people what to do."

From what he'd seen, she couldn't even get the servants in her cousin's house to obey her. So whom did she command? Her siblings? He and Edmund had certainly never let Cyril lord it over them. "Your brother really does what you tell him?"

She laughed. "No. But Louly does. She's ten, and still thinks I'm wise."

"Intelligent child. As to your brother—I've never had a sister, but I can imagine how he feels when you try to put his life in order. And he the head of the family—how old is he?"

She looked puzzled for a moment, and then rather embarrassed. "Oh. I thought you knew. But I suppose you were on the Continent when—when the scandal happened."

"Scandal?" Surely her brother would have been too young to create a scandal?

A muscle in her cheek tightened. "Tom is my stepbrother—his mother married my father when he was four, and I seven. So I think of him as my brother."

"Doesn't sound scandalous to me."

She made an impatient sound. "Did I mention the part

where my father lost the entire estate at cards, and his charming wife ran off to Italy with a younger man? A younger man with money, of course. It's always money, isn't it?"

He couldn't blame her for the bitter tone in her voice. "She left her children?"

"Oh, she liked them well enough. She just liked luxury more."

He felt for them. "So you have the raising of your siblings?"

"I haven't the money." Frustration made her voice rough. "I managed to prep Tom so that he won a King's Scholarship at Eton, but he has neither the taste nor the aptitude for books. I knew it from the beginning, really. But what else was there?"

Here was yet another Atalanta. First, the self-possessed card player. Then the horse lover. And now this. "And your sister?"

"She, too, has the joy of living with our relatives—the relatives my father impoverished. In one year, she became fatherless, motherless, and an unpaid nurserymaid to boot."

Her face was flushed, and her breathing heavy. "Could you take the ribbons?" she asked quietly.

"Of course." He took them from her shaking hands, impressed that she didn't slacken her hold on the reins until he had them.

As soon as her hands were free, she pressed them against her reddened cheeks. "I have no idea why I told you all that." She took a deep breath of the crisp air. "I never babble on like that, never. I do beg your pardon."

"You have nothing to apologize for. I would feel the same in your shoes."

"They wouldn't fit you." She gave a strangled laugh. "Sorry. I hope I didn't upset Lucifer and Rogue."

"They're happy as grigs."

"Thank you." She leaned back against the cushions and breathed slowly, as if trying to restore her calm.

He mulled over for a bit what she had told him. Eventually, he said, "Tom is your stepbrother, and Louly is your half sister?"

"That's right."

"We were three as well, before Cyril died. You see, I've only been an eldest sibling for a little more than a year, so I'm not as proficient at it as you. I couldn't make Edmund study Greek if I tried."

She gave a soft smile. "Edmund was the young man you rescued from Lady Isabella's? He didn't remind me of you at all."

He nodded at an acquaintance as they passed a cluster of open carriages. "I suppose that's what the cavalry does— changes you beyond all recognition."

"Oh, you were in a cavalry regiment?" She sounded pleased. "I should have known, you love horses so."

Of course, it wasn't so simple. "That's the best thing about being in the cavalry, and the worst. You and your horse develop a communication like none other." Seeing Lucifer distracted by a playful dog off to the side, he pulled up slightly on the reins. "The bad part is, you always have—" He broke off, trying to think how to put it nicely. "You always have higher casualty rates with the horses than the men. And that's . . . hard to bear sometimes."

She sat quietly for a minute. "I can imagine," she finally said, her voice soft. "I had a horse once. Minerva. She was such a beautiful creature, so responsive." She smiled sadly. "When I was a child, I imagined we could read each other's thoughts."

He nodded his head. "I know how that is."

"She was a splendid jumper. And her paces!" She gazed at his horses, her eyes full of longing. "I do miss her."

He saw her hands grasped tightly together in her lap, and

he wanted to do something. Comfort her, rescue her—he didn't know what.

He wasn't used to having feelings like this. "Why did you name her Minerva? Was she wise among horses?"

That brought a twinkle to her eye. "I was not so besotted with her that I imagined her wiser than any other horse. No, she had a shield-shaped star on her forehead, and I thought it looked like Minerva's shield."

He caught his breath. A shield-shaped star. How common could that be? "What did she look like?" he asked, trying to keep his voice matter-of-fact.

"She was a deep red chestnut, very elegant. As well as the star, she had one white sock, and a tiny snip over her left nostril. She had perfect feet, too—even her white foot never gave me any problem."

Good God. He felt like he'd been hit by a mortar round.

She didn't seem to notice. "Tom's horse was a bay gelding named Icarus. He seemed to think he could fly—the horse did, I mean," she added with a smile in her voice. "Even Tom wasn't that madcap." She paused, and then said in a sadder tone, "At least, he wasn't that madcap in those days. Sometimes I think something changed in him when we lost everything."

He couldn't let her see how much she'd shocked him. He took his chaotic thoughts in an iron grip, much as he had so often on the battlefield. "I've known horses who thought they could fly. They can make terrific jumpers if they keep their feet up."

She sighed. "Icarus didn't have Minerva's grace, but he had plenty of spirit. Tom was so broken up when we had to let the horses go."

So that was it. He should have known. "When your father lost his money, he sold your horses?"

"He had to," she said quickly. "We all knew that. He had so many debts, and the horses were among his greatest as-sets." She made an irritated sound. "It sounds so cold. As-sets. But that's what they were, I suppose."

She took a deep breath. "Of course," she said, her voice slightly more cheerful, "the bright side of it is that I know they must be very well taken care of wherever they are now. They're worth too much not to be."

He kept his eyes forward. "To whom did your father sell the horses?"

"We never knew—all he would say was he'd found them a good home. He thought it would be easier for us not to know, I suppose. And before I got up the nerve to ask him where they'd gone, he—he passed on."

"I'm sorry." It was such an inadequate thing to say. I'm sorry. As if he'd trod on her skirt.

He'd done much worse than that. If his suspicion was correct, his family had done Atalanta an injury she might never be able to forgive.

Hearing a bee buzzing next to her ear, Atalanta gave a start. How long had she been sitting here in Stoke's curricle, absorbed in her thoughts? She glanced around at the length-ening shadows of the trees and, feeling cold air nipping at the bare skin of her neck, realized that evening was coming.

What was wrong with her? The Park was fresh and brim-ming with life, but all she could think about was death—the death of her father, her family, her sense of security.

And the death of her dreams. Even though he'd lost their entire estate, while her father had lived, something in her be-lieved that he would find a way to rescue them all.

She hadn't faced the truth until the pneumonia had finally claimed his broken spirit. Then she knew: It was her task to rescue Tom and Louly. There was no one else to fight for them, to protect them.

To avenge them. "Will you be at Lady Isabella's gathering tomorrow night?" she asked Lord Stoke, the image of Louly's pale face lingering in her memory.

"Lady Isabella's?" He sounded startled. "Well, I—wait, that reminds me. Here." He handed her the reins and reached into a coat pocket.

He trusted her. He must, to hand her the reins so casually, with such valuable horses. Horses he clearly cared about.

Her stomach churned. No, she couldn't be weak. For Tom and Louly's sake, she couldn't.

"Here are your winnings," he said, pulling some coins out of his pocket. "Fifteen shillings."

The coins felt cold, even through her glove. "Thank you."

He took back the reins. "Oh, and—no. I don't think I shall be at Lady Isabella's."

She kept her eyes on Rogue's glossy ears. "Don't forget, you promised me a rematch."

She could see him glance at her, then look away. "Did I?"

"Just now, at my cousin's house."

She could see the tension in his strong hands, but his hold on the reins never altered. "Ah yes, I suppose I did."

Why did she feel so contemptible? She had no choice. "You may as well play me at Lady Isabella's. I shall be there, and you're one of the few piquet players I know in town."

There. Now she felt lower than a worm. He would recall that Malkham might be there, and his protective instincts would be roused.

She could see a muscle in his jaw tighten. "Very well. I shall be there."

She felt her heart leap.

Oh, no. This couldn't be. She didn't care for him, did she? What a cruel joke. That could ruin everything she'd worked for, fought for, prayed for all these years.

But when she thought of seeing him again so soon, she

suddenly felt she had something to look forward to. Someone to talk to.

This would never do.

She clenched her hands in her lap, reminding herself to be strong. "I'm so pleased," she said, fighting to keep her tone light. "I do love winning."

He shifted on the seat. "Don't forget you can lose, too."

"I won't. Lose, that is."

She could see the muscle in his jaw tighten again. "Gaming is a dangerous business, Miss James, and those who fail to take it seriously often suffer greatly by it. You of all people should know that."

He was throwing her father at her? How dare he. "And so should you," she shot back.

"I?" His voice held surprise, and perhaps a hint of . . . guilt? "Why do you say that?"

"Your father was as noted a gamester as mine."

"Well, yes, but my father didn't . . ."

She clenched her hands so hard they hurt. "He didn't bankrupt his family? No. But as you were saying, that was just luck, wasn't it? The turn of the card, as they say?"

He made an irritated sound in his throat. "Perhaps."

"And perhaps I am perfectly able to take care of myself."

The muscle in his jaw twitched. "Of course." His voice was cold. "I beg your pardon, Miss James. I shall not make the mistake of trying to protect you again."

The air was colder now as they made their way through the crowd of carriages at Hyde Park Corner, and Atalanta shivered a little.

As Stoke turned the curricle into Park Lane, she found herself beset by confused thoughts. Why did she feel so low? This was what she wanted, wasn't it? To be at odds with Lord Stoke? To no longer have him watching out for her?

Then why did she have a strong urge to cry?

Chapter Five

*T*he warm smell of hay blended with the pungent scent of horses and leather, and for the first time in weeks Stoke felt like he was home. Of course, the mews behind his London townhouse bore only passing resemblance to his stables in the country. Even if he couldn't see the red brick walls that bounded him in on all sides, he would know he was in London by the acrid coal smoke in the air.

He stroked Lucifer's neck and waited. He'd never known his father's head groom all that well, but he noted the calloused hands and wrinkled red face that proclaimed O'Flaherty's long years spent caring for the horses of Stoke.

If anyone knew, it was O'Flaherty.

"How long ago, you said?" asked the man, absently shooing a fly away from Lucifer's gleaming black coat.

What had she said? "Five years, or thereabouts. The mare had a white snip over one nostril, and a shield-shaped star on her forehead."

O'Flaherty scratched his chin. "Sounds right. The ones your da sent you overseas, now, weren't they?"

He felt a tension in his chest. "That's right—the chestnut and the bay. And a roan, I think. I can't find any records of my father buying them."

The groom smiled to reveal several missing teeth. "No,

that you wouldn't, lad." The man blinked for a second, and his grin widened. "Beg pardon. *Milord*. Seems strange, calling you that. Guess I'm used to calling the earl that. I mean to say—the last earl, your father."

The man was about as fast as dried treacle. "Don't worry about it. Just tell me—do you know where the purchase records are?"

O'Flaherty picked up a brush, stared at it for a moment, then started currying Lucifer's already pristine back at a leisurely pace. "Weren't no records."

No records? That was careless, even for his father. "Do you know from whom he bought them?"

"Oh, they weren't bought."

It was like questioning the Sphinx. "Not bought? What does that mean?"

The ruddy-faced man shrugged. "Gentleman owed him money. Gave him the horses instead."

Stoke felt his stomach plummet. "Who was it?" The groom threw him a curious look, as if he felt the line of questioning was unusual. Of course it was, but Stoke no longer cared about tact. His patience was wearing thin.

"James, it was."

"Viscount James?"

O'Flaherty nodded calmly. "The horse-breeding one. Bred the Derby winner three years in a row, did you know? Few years back, like. Prime horseflesh, that was."

Restraining an urge to grab the man by the shoulders and shake some speed into him, Stoke ran a hand through his close-cropped hair. "Why did the viscount owe my father money?"

O'Flaherty wrinkled his jaw about, and for a moment, it looked like he was chewing his cud. "Dunno. But we got more than them three thoroughbreds, I know that. Good deal of breeding stock." He patted Lucifer's shining black coat.

"Not you, young feller," he told the horse. "But a whole passel o' your stablemates, wasn't it?"

He had to be certain. "Including the horses my father sent me in Spain?"

The man nodded slowly. "Yup. That I do remember. Had a hell of a time transportin' them—pardon my language, sir. But there it is."

His luck was out. Until this moment he hadn't quite believed it, but there it was, staring him in the face.

Only one thing could be worse. And as soon as Edmund came home from whatever indulgence he was wallowing in, Stoke would learn the truth. Brotherly kindness be damned.

"Are you sure this is the address?" Atalanta asked her stepbrother, peering down the dank alley off Broad Court. Greenish-brown bricks covered with patches of grime were partly obscured by random heaps of rubbish that looked like they'd been there a long time.

Tom consulted the tattered paper in his hand. "Supposed to be. Cousin of his lives on Curzon Street in Mayfair, but rumor has it Sir Geoffrey hasn't even visited there in years. No, he should be here—right after the public house, it says." He frowned in puzzlement. "Down the alley, perhaps?"

It looked bad enough now, with the morning sun throwing a bit of light into the filthy area. How would it look in the dark of evening? The drooping doorways could hide pickpockets, or worse.

Could Sir Geoffrey Yarrow be living in a place like this? "You're certain?"

Tom groaned. "Look, this is the best information I have. Take it or leave it."

She clenched her hands together nervously over her reticule. "Let's get it over with."

She followed Tom gingerly across the slippery, uneven

bricks, past the piles of refuse and thick ash. The alley ended in a mud-colored wall, but just before the end she saw a heavy wooden door.

They climbed up on the step in front of it. The sooty side of the building leaned over them ominously, dampness dripping off the blackened bricks.

"Want me to pound on the door?" Tom's voice was too cheerful. That meant he was scared.

"Go ahead," she said, trying to sound calm.

He made his hand into a fist and hammered on the thick wood.

She could hardly hear the sound. "I don't suppose there's a bell?" She looked around, but saw nothing of the kind. Which, she supposed, was only to be expected. Narrow alleyways didn't get many callers, did they?

Tom stuck his hands in his pockets as he waited, shifting his weight from one foot to the next.

A chill breeze whistled between the buildings, and Atalanta shivered. "Why don't you knock again?"

Tom pounded again on the heavy door, and they waited.

Was that a creak? It was hard to separate it from the traffic noises coming from Pall Mall, but she thought it sounded like the creak of an old staircase.

Apparently Tom heard it too, for he pounded with renewed vigor. The creak was clearer this time, accompanied by a rhythmic thumping.

She heard the scraping of a bolt being drawn back, and then the wooden door opened a crack.

A bloodshot eye peered out at them. "What do you want?" grated the quavering voice of an aged man.

She stepped forward. "I'm looking for Sir Geoffrey Yarrow. Does he live here?"

The eye stared at her balefully. "What do you want?" the voice repeated.

She stood straight and tall. "I am Miss Atalanta James,"

she said, trying to sound imperious. "I am the daughter of
Augustus, Viscount James, and I wish to speak with Sir
Geoffrey."

The eye blinked a few times. "What for?" grated the
voice.

The breeze chilled the back of her neck. "That is between
Sir Geoffrey and me."

"Well he doesn't want to see you." The eye disappeared
and the door started to close. Just in time, Tom threw himself against it.

This wasn't working. She hadn't intended to show her
hand yet, but it looked like she had no choice.

She raised her voice. "I need to see him. Tell him I have
a card."

"Don't want your card."

She took a deep breath of frigid air. "A playing card," she
said, tightening her chest to keep her voice steady. "Tell him
I have a playing card, and if he doesn't see me, he will learn
what regret feels like."

Tom staggered as the door fell open inward.

An elderly man stood hunched in the doorway. His pale
skin hung loose from his bony face, just as his purple brocade dressing gown hung from his angular frame.

The clothes told her that this was no servant. "Sir Geoffrey Yarrow, I presume?"

The man pulled his lips back in what looked like a gri-
mace. "Are you the James girl?"

She drew herself up. "Yes. I want to play cards with
you."

He coughed, or laughed, or something. "Like father, like
daughter? What, haven't the James family lost enough yet?
They want to give me more?"

He stepped back. "Come in, come in," he said, waving
them forward. "Come into my palace."

Her gaze flickered to Tom, who gave her a little nod. Well, if Tom wasn't afraid, neither was she.

Pulling her skirt close to keep it clean, she stepped over the grimy threshold. As soon as Tom followed her in, she heard the man bang the door shut and draw the bolt.

Good Lord, it *was* a palace. Or a pirate's cave. She could hardly see through dim, smoky candlelight, but in the room behind Sir Geoffrey she observed a clutter of elaborate clocks, porcelain dishes, and what looked like ivory carvings. Stacks of paintings leaned against delicate satin-covered chairs, all covered by thick layers of dust.

Sir Geoffrey waved a bony hand at the room. "She wants some of it, hmm? Wants to play me for it?"

She felt Tom standing next to her, his sturdy presence comforting in this eerie place. "I want to play piquet with you," she said. "I like piquet."

"The girl likes piquet." A dry laugh shook his sere body. "Likes piquet, eh? So did her father. Before he lost. Oh yes, lost everything."

He stepped close to her, and in the flickering candlelight she could see that both of his eyes were bloodshot. "I'm no fool. Not I. James thinks he'll get it all back? Too late. Years too late. It's mine now. Mine."

She felt Tom shift beside her. He was probably nervous—heavens, she could hardly keep from running herself.

"I wish to play cards with you, sir," she said. "Imagine the scandal if certain things were to come to light."

"Light? Light?" He peered around the room, as if confused. "No light in here, James, not in here. No one comes in here but Jack. Won't catch me with that one. I'm safe here, nothing can touch me."

Shaking his head, he backed away. "Nothing. And no one. Not even James." His voice faded away. "Not even James. Dead now, dead and quiet. Can't touch me."

Was he mad? She didn't have much experience with such things, but though he talked strangely, he seemed to understand everything she said.

In for a penny, in for a pound. "I can touch you," she said, keeping her voice low but steady. "I am my father's daughter, and what he knew, I know too. You cannot ignore that."

His eyes narrowed and he scowled, exposing a row of crooked yellowing teeth. "Spying on me, are you? Creeping in and spying? Get out! I won't let you creep about and steal from me. Not James. Not anyone."

He strode to the exit, pulled the protesting bolt, and flung open the door. "Out!"

Edmund stared in vague confusion. "What time is it?"

Stoke took in his younger brother's slightly uneven walk and realized he'd been drinking. No surprise there, considering it was one in the morning. He was just glad tonight hadn't been one of Edmund's all-night revels. "I wanted to talk to you."

Edmund blinked at the lamp in Stoke's hand. "Now? Can't it wait?"

"This evening would have been agreeable, but you weren't here. So now will have to do."

Edmund grumbled, but he followed his brother into the library. "I wasn't playing hazard, if that's what you're going to ask."

"It isn't." Stoke sat behind the desk and indicated a chair. "There are things that happened when I was in the Peninsula, and I need information on them. You were likely too young for Father or Cyril to have confided in you, but I expect you know more than I do."

Edmund flopped down tiredly into a chair. "Fire away."

Stoke scowled at the stack of yellowing papers in front of him. "About five years ago, the previous Viscount James owed Father a sizable sum. As at least part of the payment, James gave him some horses. What do you know about it?"

Edmund fiddled with his tight cravat. "Five years ago?" He thought for a second, then gave Stoke a sheepish look. "I'm not in the briars, then?"

A grin tugged at Stoke's mouth. "No, you're not in trouble. Not this time. Just tell me what you know."

Edmund frowned in thought. "James? Don't think I ever met him."

"Probably not—I think he died soon after."

"Really?" Edmund's eyes narrowed. "No, wait—you're talking about Atalanta James's father, aren't you? You're still pursuing her?"

Why did he feel so guilty? "I'm not pursuing her, I'm just . . ." What was he doing? "Listen, Edmund—it looks as if when Lord James lost his whole estate at cards, Father was one of the parties he lost it to."

Edmund whistled. "Didn't know that. So dear Papa ruined your inamorata's father? Tricky, that."

"She's not my—" Seeing his brother's grin, he broke off. "Did anyone ever tell you you're annoying as hell?"

"Often. Especially the ladies."

"I can believe it." He scratched at his jaw. "Do you remember when we got India and Beau Walker?"

"Hmm . . ." Edmund frowned for a second. "I suppose it was about five years ago, now that you mention it. They were James horses?"

"Those, and others. Good God, the bulk of the Stoke stables seems to have come from that one damned card game."

"If you want to be certain, you can always write to the Jockey Club. They keep records on all the thoroughbreds."

"I didn't think of that. Good idea."

"You know, that could explain a lot of things," Edmund said meditatively. "Some of the older fellows—well, they've made certain remarks I never understood. Might have been referring to that game, now that I think of it. And another thing—could explain why we've never had adequate histories on several of the mares. That's annoying, you know."

Here was a new side to Edmund. "I didn't realize you were interested in the stables."

Edmund shrugged. "It's hard not to be, growing up a Stanton."

That was true. What's more, it might just be the key to solving the problem of what to do with Edmund.

But he had to think it through first. "I was in the Peninsula when the whole thing happened, but I'm surprised no one mentioned it."

Edmund began to untie his cravat. "Didn't it take forever to get a letter to you? I expect Father just forgot about the whole thing by the next time he wrote you."

That was hard to believe. "In any case, I don't know what to do about this."

"Do about it? Why should you do anything about it?"

"Why?" He could hardly believe his ears. "Why? A good deal of our prosperity was gained by impoverishing an entire family. Atalanta—Miss James—is in an untenable position, living with uncaring relatives, unable to provide for her siblings as she would wish."

He got up from the desk and began pacing around the dusty room. "And to top it all, we have their horses. The James stables were famous—everyone knows their name. And now I learn our stables have made their name on the ruin of a good family?"

"We did not." Edmund tore off his cravat. "Our horses have been first-rate for as long as I can remember—you know that. Perhaps they were improved by James stock—I won't deny it. But no gentleman has the right to sit down at the gaming table without being ready to lose what he wagers."

Stoke brushed at his hair impatiently. "I know that. Believe me, Edmund, I know that. But—it's wrong. It has to be."

Edmund shrugged. "Those are the risks. We all know them. Why, that's what makes betting exciting."

"But the family takes the same risk, without any choice in the matter, don't they? The James children didn't ask to have a gamester for a father, or to have their inheritance wagered for a fleeting thrill. How can it be right to take the stake in such a case? It's like forcing rents from a starving family. It can't be right."

Edmund loosened his collar. "But what can you do? What's done is done, and it was done years ago, too. If it comes in your way to do a favor for the family, that can't do any harm. But what more can they expect?"

He paced across the room, his mind running in frustrating circles. "I don't know that they expect anything. Hell, I don't think they have any idea where the money went. They couldn't have been more than children." Atalanta would have been, what? Thirteen or thereabouts?

What was he doing at thirteen? Shirking his studies and haunting the stables, playing tricks on their starchy butler and tagging along with Cyril whenever he could.

How would he have felt to have lost it all in one day? And they'd lost more than that—they'd lost their father and mother as well.

Now Edmund was talking about doing a random, casual favor? "I owe them more than that."

Edmund leaned back in the chair and sighed. "You owe them nothing."

He turned to face his brother. "If you really believe that, you're not the man I think you are."

Edmund looked sulky. "You don't know anything about it. You give me a great speech about our precious family and our holy name, but what do you do? Spend your time fighting abroad, and when you finally come home, you're more interested in taking care of some chit you just met than protecting your own interests. What about us? Or are we too flat for you?"

There was no "us" anymore, of course. Only Edmund—and himself. "I'm not going to forget about my duty, Edmund. You needn't fear I'll sacrifice the good of our family trying to help Atalanta James, or anyone. Believe me—my duty here comes first. It always has."

But where did his duty lie in this case? He shook his head, wishing the answers were clearer. "I have to do something, Edmund. I can feel it. If you don't understand that, I'm sorry, but that doesn't change things."

Edmund leaned back in the chair and sighed. "Is that it, then? Am I excused to get some sleep, O lord and master?"

It was like dealing with a child. "Yes, go to bed," he said, a reluctant smile on his face. "Get the sweet sleep of the innocent. One day you'll have responsibilities weighing you down too, and you'll know what care is. You may as well sleep while you can."

Edmund gave him a mock salute. "Aye, aye, sir. Sleep duty for me, sir. At once, your supreme lordiness."

Stoke advanced on his brother as if he meant to throw him out of the room. "Get out, brat! And learn the difference between the army and the navy before you mock your elders."

"I defer to you, O decrepit one." Edmund swept his brother a flourishing bow, then ran up the stairs with the careless energy of youth.

It must be heaven to have no worries. To have nothing weighing on your chest every night, and weighing just as heavily the next morning.

But he'd never questioned his fate, and there was no point starting now. He had more important things to wrestle with.

Such as what to do about Miss Atalanta James.

Chapter Six

$\mathcal{A}$talanta sat on a bench in St. James's Park the next morning, feeling the stiff breeze tugging at the brim of her bonnet. Ducks swam past along the shimmering lake, birds and squirrels begged for bread, but she gave them no notice.

What was she to do? Tom sprawled next to her on the bench, his normally cheerful face downcast. He was her responsibility, even if there was no blood connection. She had to provide for him. "Don't worry," she said, laying her hand on his arm. "This is only a minor setback. I have plenty of contingency plans."

She opened the reticule on her lap and took out the pack of cards it held.

Tom groaned. "Not again! How much more practice do you need? You're already perfect."

Atalanta started dealing out the cards. "There's no such thing."

"Yes there is! I know I'm perfectly sick of helping you practice. It's perfectly dull and perfectly tedious to play cards with someone who can read your mind and know every card you've got."

"I don't read your mind." Atalanta finished dealing, and picked up her cards. "I read your actions."

"Dashed if I know how!"

That made her grin. "Practice, of course. Practice makes perfect, don't you know."

"Don't I!" he said, in a pained voice. He made his discards, and she took the remaining three cards.

It was so easy. "You have six hearts, ace high, but you're missing the knave and the nine. I know your spades and clubs, too, but I can't yet say whether your king of diamonds is protected. That I'll know with the first card you play."

He threw down his cards in disgust. "That's it. You don't need any more practice. You've spent years improving your game, analyzing every hand—you're ready, Atalanta. You've been ready for years. But that's not the problem."

Atalanta collected the scattered cards. "The plan is on track," she said, with more confidence than she felt. "I'm certain we'll work out whatever little snags we hit."

He looked up, but his eyes weren't hopeful. "Are you? Sir Geoffrey won't talk to you. You need time to work on Malkham. And you haven't even found Stoke yet."

The words hurt, and she had to look away. "I suppose I forgot to mention it, but—it seems I actually have met Lord Stoke. I didn't know who he was at first, you see."

Tom sat up. "That's good news."

Of course it was. So why did she feel anything but good? "And I expect to play Malkham in a few days," she said slowly, placing the cards back into her reticule and slowly tightening the drawstring. "I'll just have to move up the schedule."

Tom pushed his hair back from his forehead. "That's a risk, isn't it? That doesn't sound like you."

No, it didn't. "Sometimes you have to gamble."

And sometimes you had to sacrifice. She thought she'd become inured to it, but hurting Stoke would be a sacrifice unlike any she had ever made.

She'd always been so sure she was in the right. But now

she was hiding things from Tom. That was a bad sign. Was she compromising her loyalties?

She couldn't afford to. She knew where her duty lay. Every day for the past six years she'd worked toward this. She had no right to let her emotions get in the way.

Stoke walked meditatively up Chandler Street. He was glad he'd decided to walk to see Miss James. The day was unseasonably warm, and after all his years in Spain, he wasn't used to being cooped up inside all the time.

The houses here were smaller than most in Mayfair, though he knew they still must be worth a pretty penny. Atalanta's family probably owned their townhouse, shabby as it was. If they were like many others, they rented it out during most of the year, and only came up to London for one month during the spring season. It was a common enough story for aristocratic families fallen on hard times.

He felt a tightening in his chest. His father had borne some guilt for bringing those hard times down on Atalanta's family. Now, as his father's heir, he carried it as well.

But what could he do? He was in a damnable position, feeling responsible for their situation, but without the right to fix it. He would do what he could, but even that might create scandal.

Then again, the Goddess of the Cards did not seem overly concerned with creating a scandal. Perhaps her past had inured her to scandal. On the other hand, it could be that she was counting on the fact that a viscount's daughter could get away with a good many things that less high-born misses would be shunned for.

He turned the corner onto Bird Street, and there she was. In the warm sun, she looked young and vulnerable. A tendril of golden hair escaped her bonnet and lay lightly on her shoulder. She was all in blue again, and for a moment he thought she looked like spring.

Which was ridiculous, of course. She looked like a well-bred lady, and nothing else.

She was rapt in conversation with an energetic young boy about her own height—her stepbrother, perhaps? The lad's curly brown hair stuck out at all angles, and his clothes were creased. Wouldn't the servants press his clothes? Or was he living elsewhere?

As he drew near them, he saw the boy hand Atalanta a folded note. It looked like she was about to read it when she noticed his approach.

She looked up at him. He could see recognition dawn, and for a moment her eyes lit up and it looked to him like she was about to smile.

Did she feel it, then—this kinship? He'd only known her a few days, but she was already a presence in his life. And with her lonely circumstances, it would not be surprising if she felt the same about him.

He tipped his hat. "Good day, Miss James. Would you care for a ride in the Park this afternoon?"

She did smile at him now, but the spontaneous warmth was gone. "Good day to you, too." She turned away slightly, and he saw her slip the note into the pocket of her pelisse.

The boy grinned at him, and Stoke waited for her to introduce them.

Instead, she leaned toward the boy. "I'll see you tomorrow, then."

Perhaps she didn't think he would condescend to be introduced to her schoolboy stepbrother. He turned to the boy and held out his hand. "How do you do? I'm Stoke."

The boy's brown eyes widened, and he made no attempt to shake Stoke's hand. He glanced at his sister, then back at the earl. "Stoke? You're Lord Stoke?"

Stoke blinked, his memory suddenly jogged. Hadn't Atalanta reacted strangely to his name, too? And now her brother. Could they know his father had helped bankrupt theirs?

He nodded at the boy. "I am. Do you know me?"

The boy flushed. "No. I'm Tom." He glanced at Atalanta again. "I didn't know you were friends with my sister."

At that, Atalanta laid her hand on her brother's arm. "I told you we'd met. Thank you for coming to see me, Tom."

Her tone was clearly a dismissal. Tom's nostrils flared, and he thrust his chin forward at his sister. "You sure you want to see me tomorrow?"

Atalanta's grip on her brother's arm tightened visibly. "Of course I do." Her tone was light, but he could see the tension in her shoulders. She gave her brother a pat. "Now don't waste any more time on me, or you'll keep Percy waiting."

Tom tilted his head to one side. "Wouldn't want that, would we now?" He gave Atalanta a cold nod and turned away. He jumped down into the street and galloped across the road, nearly being run over by a cart in the process.

What was that all about? Clearly something they didn't want him to know about. "I hope I didn't intrude."

She turned back to him with a flushed face. "Oh, no— that was nothing. Tom has a few peculiarities, and a—a somewhat uneven temper. He doesn't mean anything by it."

"I understand," he said, though he didn't. "You don't need to make excuses for him—I don't offend easily."

A faint smile touched her lips. "I'm glad."

She hadn't said anything about his invitation to go riding, he noticed. She might have just been distracted by her brother, of course.

But she might still be angry at him. He'd nearly forgotten that they hadn't parted on friendly terms. She might not care for his company.

Perhaps that was why there was a strange feeling in his stomach. "Would you like to go riding, Miss James?"

She glanced into the street. "Riding? Where are your horses?"

"I didn't want to leave them standing in the street while

you changed." Suddenly, that struck him as an indelicate thing to say. He felt his neck grow hot under his cravat. "That is—if you wished to wear a habit. . . ."

This was ridiculous. He was no callow boy. So why was he blushing?

He could see laughter in her eyes. "How kind of you to ask me riding, Lord Stoke." The corners of her mouth turned up, showing the small dimple in her left cheek. "And I shall be pleased to, ah, change my clothes to try out your horse."

Minx. He could tell she was laughing at him. "My groom and I shall return in, what? A quarter hour?"

"That will be ample." She inclined her head, a teasing glint in her eye. "My habit and I shall be waiting for you."

He could feel the warmth rise from his neck to his face. Women.

Though this one might be more of a mystery than most. And if he could keep his mind off the image of her in her underclothes, he might be able to figure that mystery out.

She shouldn't be so pleased. For years she had planned how to ruin the Earl of Stoke, and now all she could think about was the fact that he wanted to go riding with her.

Her sole riding habit was only marginally presentable, as socializing hadn't been a priority in her grand plan. She stared at herself in the pier glass and frowned. The carefully made-over garment gapped at her waist and was noticeably shiny at the elbows, if one knew where to look. But if Stoke liked her, he shouldn't care about such things.

Liked her? Indeed.

She was going to end up like the mythical Atalanta if she went on in this way. When, as a child, she'd finally learned the true story of the legend of Atalanta, she'd been painfully disappointed. How could it be that such a fierce princess, the fastest runner in the world, should have lost her fateful race because she let a golden apple distract her from her aim? A silly golden apple, tossed in her path by a man who could not outrun her fairly?

Atalanta had hated her name for a while after learning that story. Then she'd decided that she would be the Atalanta who should have been. She would ignore any golden apples in her path, and just keep running.

She was no longer a child, but she still felt the same way. She must let nothing turn her from her goal. The end was now in sight, and all she had to do was keep striving for it. If she gave up now—abandoned Tom and Louly because she lacked the courage or will to fight for them—she might as well give up living, too. For what was the point of life if you just allowed fate to buffet you about, and never even tried?

These thoughts were still whirling about in her head when she made her way down the stairs. She was glad she had run into Lord Stoke on the street, rather than having him call here. This way, she could avoid a possibly embarrassing scene with Cousin Harriet.

But it was too bad that Tom had been there. The memory of how he had reacted to Stoke was not pleasant. Of course, she hadn't told him about Stoke. What was there to tell? But Tom clearly felt she'd deceived him. Or at least failed to confide in him.

Well, she would apologize tomorrow and explain everything. Now was her chance to study Stoke, to put him off his guard, so when they next played piquet, her path would be clear. Tom's expulsion from Eton meant that she was running out of time. She should be happy for this chance to hurry her scheme with Stoke.

And that was all she should be happy for.

Atalanta stepped outside the house. She'd hurried so that she'd arrive before Stoke, thus making it unnecessary for him to be noticed by her relatives—or to notice them.

Just as she pulled the door closed behind her, she saw Stoke riding around the corner. He was so at ease on the horse, they almost looked like one creature. A centaur, perhaps. Were all cavalry officers so striking?

He held his head high, and his posture was straight but comfortable. His mount was a striking gray, proud and responsive. And the horse his groom led was a beauty, too—a graceful chestnut that reminded her of her treasured Minerva.

Her throat grew tight. Had he recalled her confidences, and brought this horse because of its resemblance to her long-gone mare?

Her eyes prickled. Why did life have to be so difficult, so complicated? She'd thought her choices were easy, but they were becoming more difficult by the hour.

Adjusting her bonnet, she stepped to the curb. When Stoke saw her he smiled, and she felt herself smiling in response.

He indicated the chestnut. "Will Keemun suit?"

She moved to the mare's head and stroked her satiny nose. "Beautifully."

With athletic grace, he dismounted his tall horse and handed the reins to the groom. "I thought you would enjoy a ride in the Park on such a pleasant day." He moved to the near side of the mare. "May I help you up?"

She gave the horse and saddle a quick, assessing glance and moved toward Stoke. He smelled of leather and saddle oil, and she had a sudden impulse to bury her face in his soft woolen coat and breathe in his scent.

She looked up at his tanned face and caught her breath. He was so near that she could have leaned against him.

She didn't feel like herself. He held out his hands to help her into the saddle, and she felt her skin prickle.

Hoping he didn't notice her discomposure, she placed her booted foot in his hands and let him lift her up.

She spent the next minute arranging her skirts and getting the feel of the reins, and by the time he'd remounted his horse, she felt more in command of herself.

He tossed a coin to the red-coated groom. "Have a tankard on me."

The groom set off, presumably for the nearest public house. Stoke pulled his horse up beside hers. "Are you settled?"

"Yes, thank you." She couldn't meet his gaze for long, so she leaned forward and stroked the mare's neck. "What did you say her name was?"

He smiled affectionately at the horse. "Keemun, because she's the color of the tea. Shall we go?"

He led the way toward Park Lane, slowly at first, so she could get a feel for the horse, and the horse for her.

It felt good to be riding again, and she heaved a deep sigh of contentment.

He looked over at her. "How long has it been since you sat a horse?"

"Am I doing that badly?"

He gave her an amused look. "You know that's not what I meant."

"I know." She dropped the mare's head to let her see a brick in the road. "And yes, it has been some time. I feel quite—different." That wasn't what she'd meant to say, but she couldn't think of any word that covered everything that was running through her mind. And if she could, she wouldn't dare say it.

They made their way carefully through Hyde Park Corner past high-stepping carriage horses and restless mounts. As they approached Rotten Row, Stoke drew his horse up. "Why don't we ride on one of the other paths today? When I'm away from the crush, I almost feel I'm in the country. And there may even be room for a gallop."

It sounded heavenly. "You don't need to convince me. Which way?"

He turned to the right, and they made their way past a grove of arching trees. "Do you want to try out her paces?"

She couldn't resist. "I'll take good care of her," she said.

She adjusted the reins, felt Keemun's mouth, and nudged her back into a trot.

When she thought she'd found the horse's rhythm well enough, she moved her into a canter. The air whistled past her ears, and she felt more powerful than she had in a long time. It was like being a young girl again, with no worries except which hill to explore next.

The path ahead was clear and straight, so she nudged Keemun into a gallop.

Oh, what she wouldn't give to hunt again, to jump, to race across the fields every day. She couldn't think how she'd lived all these years without it.

She remembered when she hadn't thought she could survive losing Minerva and the others. Her hot, silent tears had upset her father, she could tell—but she couldn't hold them back, any more than Tom could control his frantic outbursts.

She slowed Keemun to a canter, then a trot. She was well into the Park now, and she felt like she was lost deep in a forest. Birds thronged in the trees around her, and there wasn't a building or coster in sight.

If she stuck to her guns, she could have her old life back. Even better, she could give it all back to Tom and Louly. She'd sworn she wouldn't abandon them, wouldn't give up. Her father had surrendered to what he considered the inevitable— bankruptcy and ruin, and finally death.

But at fourteen, she'd been too fierce to give up. Her father might not have had the passion to continue the fight, but she did. She would not let the world trample on her family. She would fight it, and win.

She slowed the mare and circled her around to face the way they'd come. She kept her at a walk for a bit, reluctant to return to the real world. She knew that running away from her problems was no solution, but every now and then she grew tired of the constant struggle, and wanted to retreat to her little room and forget her troubles.

But she never allowed herself to indulge in such thoughts for long. She soon gave Keemun the signal to trot, then urged her to a canter.

When she drew up in front of Stoke, she was struck again by how different he was from anyone she'd ever known. He could be so kind, but she always sensed an implacable will underneath everything he did and said. He would be a strong ally, but perhaps an even more dangerous foe.

But she refused to be daunted.

His eyes twinkled at her, and she realized that her braids had come loose. "Did you enjoy your ride?" he said.

She leaned forward to pat the mare. "She's a splendid beast. Are all your horses this fine?"

"Well, I—" He looked disconcerted for a moment. "My family has always loved horses."

"I can see why, if Keemun is a sample of your stock."

He shifted in the saddle, then adjusted his reins. "Does she remind you of Minerva?"

"Does she—? Oh, you *did* remember." She felt warm and off-balance at the same time. "You even remember her name. Well, I expect I did ramble on about her for a long time. I hope I didn't bore you to tears."

"You didn't." He glanced away, a muscle in his cheek tightening. "She looks like Minerva, then?"

She stroked the mare's mane. "She does, rather. Her points are different, of course, but her color is remarkably similar."

He looked steadily at his horse's head. "She's yours, if you want her."

She couldn't believe what she'd heard. "Sorry?"

He shifted position again, then raised his eyes to her. He looked awkward, like Tom when he stumbled into a tearful scene. "I want you to have Keemun. I'll stable her, of course. But she's yours."

This was ridiculous. The only reason a man gave a

woman a horse was if she was his mistress, and he surely
had no delusions that she was a lightskirt.

Or was he so ignorant of the rules of polite behavior?
Perhaps soldiers didn't learn these things. "I can't take a
horse from you, if that's what you're saying."

"But I—no, of course not." He scowled at his horse's
mane. "Listen, I . . . oh, hell. Can we walk for a bit?"

He was clearly thrown off by something, to be swearing
in front of her without noticing. "If you wish," she said.
They were near enough to the riders in Rotten Row and the
nursemaids leading their charges toward the Serpentine for
it to be perfectly respectable.

With a quick movement, he swung his leg over and leapt
from the horse's back. Hooking his reins over his arm, he
strode across to the mare, put his hand on Atalanta's foot,
and unhooked her boot from the stirrup.

She almost jerked her foot back, it felt so strange, even
through the leather of her boot. But if she let him know how
he made her feel, she was lost.

As she unhooked her other leg from the saddle, he
reached up and grasped her around the waist, lifting her
down as if she weighed no more than a feather.

"There," he said as he set her down. He sounded slightly
breathless.

She turned to the mare and patted her neck, as much from
the desire to look away as any concern for the horse.
Keemun was perfectly calm, so Atalanta pulled the reins
over the mare's head and started walking down the path.

Stoke followed her, leading the gray. "Look," he said, his
voice tentative. "I have little skill at saying things the polite
way—the correct way—so I'll just have to say what I need
to say."

He looked up into the trees, then down at the path. "You
may not know it, but—" He paused. "You said once that you
knew my father had a taste for the cards."

She kept her voice steady. "Yes."

He frowned. "I have recently discovered that my father won a large sum off of yours some time ago. Five years ago or so. It seems that . . ."

So he knew—at least a part of it. She didn't know what to say.

He looked like he was struggling with a difficult burden. "It seems that my father helped to bankrupt your family."

She walked for a minute in silence, her emotions in chaos. When they finally began settling down, she realized that she was glad he knew this much. She walked on under the canopy of leaves and felt like one of her cares was eased a bit.

But only one. "He did," she said quietly. "He and two others."

"Two others?"

She debated not telling him for a moment, then gave in. The whole town seemed to know anyway. "Sir Geoffrey Yarrow."

He frowned. "One of the Yarrows of Curzon Street, isn't he? Who's the other?"

She tried to make her tone sound casual. "Lord Malkham."

"Malkham?" He sounded taken aback. "And yet you game with him?"

"Why not?" It was clearly time to change the subject. "I may win back some of my father's money, don't you think? After all, that's why you offered to give me this horse, isn't it? To pay me back in some small fashion?"

He furrowed his brow. "In a way, I suppose. I didn't personally do anything to you or your family, but as the Earl of Stoke, I bear responsibility for anything my father did before me. And I can't consider it right that he would win such a large sum off of the head of a family like that."

She took in a slow breath, feeling very strange. "So you want to give me one of your horses to make up for this?"

"No, I can't—" He paused, a frustrated expression on his face. "I can't make up for it—I know that. But what can I do?"

He patted his horse and frowned. "I feel that I have to do something. You said you missed your horse so much that I thought—I wondered if you might enjoy having Keemun."

It was hardly a practical gift, even if he were to stable the horse. And it was perhaps that very lack of practicality that made her want to cry.

She stroked Keemun's neck. It would be like heaven, having a horse like this again. Or having a horse at all.

But there were so many reasons she couldn't accept. "Your offer is kind. But you know I cannot accept a horse from you."

He knitted his brows together, and stalked onward next to her. "I'm afraid I haven't told you everything," he said finally.

What more did he know? "What do you mean?"

"Your horses . . ." He looked quite fierce, as if he were going into battle. "I was in the Peninsula at the time, and I knew nothing of it. Otherwise, I would have told you sooner. I'm not good at this sort of thing, but I don't shirk my duty."

Her chest felt tight. "Our horses? You know something about what happened to our horses?"

He finally met her gaze, though obviously with great difficulty. "My father accepted many of your family's horses in lieu of the debt that was owed, when your father couldn't raise the money."

She felt like she'd been thrown into a pool of ice water. "Oh. I never thought . . ." She didn't know what to say.

He scowled down at the path. "To be perfectly frank, I expect my father had wanted the James horses for a long time. He was very passionate about the Stoke stables. I believe your father had bred several Derby winners, and I recall from my youth that was one of my father's overriding desires."

But if the previous earl had taken their horses . . . "Do you know which ones you got?" she asked, a bubble of joy rising in her. "Were the names listed anywhere? Do you recall a mare that looked rather like Keemun, but with a shield-shaped star and one white sock?"

This was more than she'd ever hoped for. She'd dreamed of reclaiming the fortune won unjustly from her father, and of starting a new stable, but some part of her had never believed she'd see Minerva again.

Or Icarus, for that matter. Tom would be so excited.

Stoke's eyes looked uneasy. "I . . . That's why I thought you might like Keemun. It seems she had the same sire as your Minerva."

"And Minerva? You have her?"

His gaze dropped. "Look, Atalanta—Miss James—a lot of time has passed, and—"

Her chest tightened. "You didn't sell her? How could you sell her?" She knew she was being unreasonable, but she didn't think she could survive the disappointment. It had been so long since she'd hoped for anything, and now she knew why. There was no pain like that of dying hope.

"I didn't sell her."

But somehow his low tone didn't make her feel any better. "What happened to her, then?"

He looked pained. "You must understand, things happen that—life is complicated. Choices are complicated."

"I know that," she said sharply. "What happened to her?"

His expression was grim. "When we were in the Peninsula, there was a great shortage of good horses, particularly for the cavalry. Without a good horse, you don't stand a chance of winning. Or surviving, for that matter. An officer must lead his men into the charge, and if he can't trust his horse . . ."

She stared at him. "You rode Minerva? Into battle? She wasn't bred for that!"

"She practically was," he said, his face betraying his strong emotion. "Horses of that type are trained to obey the smallest command of their riders. They can run and jump and—"

"But warhorses are great big beasts, aren't they?"

"Not in the light cavalry. Look, Atalanta," he said, facing her with a pleading expression. "I know this must be very difficult for you. But if you think of what was at stake—if you think what would happen to all the people you know, to your family, if Bonaparte invaded England—"

She felt like shouting at him. "Oh, so if you hadn't stolen Minerva and taken her into battle, we'd now be overrun by the French? I don't think so. So you killed her, didn't you? She's dead, right?" She began angrily, but by the end her voice was clogged with tears.

"I'm sorry." His eyes were full of compassion, and for a brief moment she wondered if he'd had to do this before, to deliver the news of a death to the people who wanted to hear it least. She felt a twinge of guilt, realizing that her loss could never compare to such as those.

But somehow, that didn't ease her pain. She hadn't ever expected to see her horse again, so why was this so difficult?

Perhaps because she no longer had the illusion that Minerva was grazing happily somewhere.

It just wasn't fair. "So why didn't you tell me right away you'd had Minerva?" Didn't he even care? "You let me babble on about her yesterday and never said a word."

"I didn't realize. We—I knew her by a different name than Minerva."

"You changed her name?"

Perhaps sensing Stoke's tension, his horse shifted nervously. He reached up to stroke its head. "I was on the Continent when my father won the horses. Around that time, I wrote him asking that he send me whatever horses he could spare. When he did, he told me her name was Lady Luck."

Lady Luck? It was a slap in the face. The previous earl's "lucky" chance had spelled ruin for her family. "And Icarus?" Her first thought should have been for Tom, of course. She could be so selfish. "Do you have Icarus? Or—did you?"

"We did."

Oh, why? "And what am I supposed to tell him? Oh sorry, someone shot your horse?" She stopped, her throat choked by tears. She pressed her hand against her mouth, feeling so helpless. She'd always felt that forging a bond with a horse meant you were responsible for it—that it was like a member of the family. But then to sell them off like—like *things*—to be killed in a stupid war.

It just didn't make sense. "So you took our horses into battle and got them killed, and now you think you can give me any old horse and pretend nothing happened?"

She tossed Keemun's reins to him. "I won't take your thirty pieces of silver. Do you think this could make up for everything? My father's death, the absence of a mother for Tom and Louly? For the—the *humiliation* they have to endure every day? You have no idea." She could no longer keep back her tears. "No idea," she repeated, knowing she was behaving atrociously, but no longer caring.

She turned and walked blindly toward Rotten Row.

"Atalanta, wait."

She could hear the sounds of him turning both horses by himself, but she didn't care. If he wanted to play the righteous man, he could do it on his own time. She had too many things to accomplish.

And a card game to look forward to.

Chapter Seven

Stoke strode up the steps of the townhouse two at a time. He'd taken a minute to see his horses properly rubbed down and stabled, and then headed straight here. Atalanta James might think she could ignore him, but she wasn't going to ignore what he had to say. And if her relatives or their incompetent servants wouldn't let him in, they'd find out what the wrath of a Stanton looked like.

Miss James always thought she was right, didn't she? And she thought he should live in guilt for the rest of his days? What his father had done was unfortunate, yes—or worse. But *he* hadn't done it. And though he was willing to accept responsibility for making some sort of reparations to the James family, he'd be damned if he was going to crawl on his knees and beg forgiveness for his father's luck at cards.

After all, no one had forced her father to play.

He rapped the door-knocker soundly. He had to wait a minute for the same gaping footman to answer the door, but when the footman recognized his scowling countenance, things moved more quickly.

Atalanta's waspish cousin was sitting primly on the sofa when the footman showed Stoke into the drawing room.

"You've come to see dear Atalanta again, haven't you? Would you like me to fetch a pack of cards?"

"Good day to you, ma'am," was all he said. He stood by the door until Atalanta came down.

He could tell she'd been crying. Her eyes were red, and much of her face as well.

All his anger died. While he'd been worrying about balancing his books with complete precision, she'd been struggling to find a way to support her brother and sister—and failing. And Tom wasn't even her real brother, yet she took responsibility for him just the same.

He knew the feeling. "Miss James," he said. "I came to ask you to come out for a drive, but I see you are suffering from a head cold. Perhaps another day?"

Her eyes were sad. "Thank you."

Her cousin rose from the sofa. "Oh, do go, child. You might think of my nerves and go bawl your eyes out someplace where I can't hear you."

Surely she'd rather be with him than with her cousin, in spite of his flaws. "Would you care for that drive after all, Miss James?" he asked gently.

She gave him a forlorn smile. After a moment, she nodded. "Yes, I would. Thank you."

He offered her his arm, and led her out into the simple hallway. She had changed her habit, he saw, and put on the light blue gown that she'd worn earlier. He pulled the drawing room door closed behind them. "I don't actually have my carriage outside," he said. "But would you like to take a walk?"

She stood still for a moment, as if debating with herself.

"Do come," he said. "I want a chance to apologize." He stopped in surprise. He hadn't meant to say that. He hadn't come here to apologize at all. But now that he thought about it, he realized that he did need to apologize. If not for his own behavior, then for his father's.

She gave a small nod. "I'll get my bonnet."

He wondered if it would be the pale blue one again, and when she came down the stairs a few minutes later he saw that it was. For the first time it occurred to him that she might only be able to afford a few nice-looking articles of clothing. Perhaps that was why she always wore blue—so that everything she had matched everything else.

He held the door open for her, and followed her out into the now cool air. "Would you like to walk toward the Park?" he asked.

She shook her head. "I'd rather not."

Of course. She wouldn't want to be seen as she was, even with her bonnet shielding her from prying eyes. "This way, then," he said, offering her his arm again.

She laid her hand lightly in the crook of his arm, and they started slowly up the street. "I came here to defend myself," he said. After all, he'd always found the truth to be the best choice. "To tell you that you were all wrong, and I was all right. But somehow, I don't think I can do it."

She didn't say anything, just walked quietly next to him. It was a strangely comforting feeling. "Look—I do the best I can. I do what I think is right, as near as I can make it out. But sometimes I find it difficult to . . ." He wasn't sure how to put it into words. "It's a tricky thing, weighing one's competing duties, deciding which take precedence."

He heard a faint sigh from her. "It is," she said. Her voice sounded tired.

"I didn't mean to slight your feelings earlier," he told her. "I know how much one can feel for a horse. Some days, I thought my horse was all that kept me sane."

She withdrew her hand from his elbow and crossed her arms over her chest, as if to keep herself warm. "You . . . you rode Minerva in Spain?"

"I rode Icarus, it seems. I knew him as Henry's Folly, actually."

"Henry's Folly?"

He wanted to squirm. "I don't think my father's naming scheme was as elegant as yours."

She grimaced. "Augustus's Folly would be more appropriate."

He found himself wanting to touch her, to comfort her. Of course, he could do no such thing. "Don't blame your father," he said instead. "I know how—how alluring gaming can be. How tempting. And many a strong man hasn't been able to stop when he should."

She looked thoughtful. "Was your father like that?"

He cast his mind back. "I think he was, really. And my brother Cyril. And to be honest, both Edmund and I have a tendency in that direction. But I refuse to be lured into such a wasteful life. No matter how exciting it may be."

They walked in silence for a bit. After a while, she seemed to stiffen her back. "So if you didn't ride Minerva, who did?"

"A good friend of mine," he said softly, for this was what he'd come to tell her. That Minerva's life hadn't been wasted.

He brought Sebastian's face to mind. They'd been so young back then. "He was a mere cornet at the time," he told her, "just as I was. But a more honest, trustworthy man I've never known."

In truth, Sebastian had seemed more truly noble than any peer he'd met. That openhearted, redheaded runt had really changed the way he thought about things. "You could rely on Sebastian in battle. Good old Basty. And you could always trust him with a secret." He had done that, many times over. How he missed Basty. "He taught me a lot about being an officer. He was willing to give his life for any of us—or any of his men."

"And . . . did he? In the end?" Her voice was gentle.

"Yes, he did," he told her quietly. "But before that, he'd

proved his mettle time and time again. And Lady Luck—
Minerva, that is—made all the difference. You should have
seen the slug Basty was riding before my father sent the
horses."

It had all been confusion in those days. Everything was
so new, so different—and none of them were trained properly. And he, who lacked training himself, was supposed to
train the men under him? It made no sense.

It had been sink or swim, with a vengeance. "Your horses
helped so much. When you're leading your men into battle,
the most important thing is keeping their spirits up, their
morale strong. So you have to look strong."

"I see."

He knew he was making a hash of it. "And there are so
many things to be looking out for—everything you have to
be aware of in hunting, plus cannonfire and gunfire, any hint
that a line or square has broken. . . . And you need to have
eyes in the back of your head to know when your men are
going to run."

She looked startled. "Do they do that much? Run, I
mean?"

He smiled. "It's nothing like in books. Everyone runs.
The important thing is not to run first." Of course, that was
a vast oversimplification. "Then again, you do run first if
you're going to be slaughtered. Unless holding the ground
for a certain time is important enough. Then you try to stand
for as long as you can."

"It sounds horrible."

"It is, really." Of course, nothing was that simple, especially in war. "It can be exciting, I suppose. And there's no
feeling like winning a major battle." Though perhaps part of
that was the relief that one wasn't lying dead next to one's
friends and comrades.

They walked past rows of nearly identical white townhouses. After a while, they turned onto a quiet street. "I sup-

pose," she said, her voice reflective, "that we at home never think of these things. We know there's a war going on. If we have relatives in service, we read the casualty lists. We cheer for every battle won. But I don't think we really spend much time thinking how it must be for the soldiers who are there day in, day out. It can't be an every-now-and-then thing for those in the army."

"True. I think that's why I have such a difficult time adjusting to private life. In the army, everything is the army— when you sleep, what you eat, who you see. It's an odd feeling to have so much control over everything I do each day."

"I expect it's a pleasant change to have so much spare time now."

He grinned. "Actually, one has far too much spare time when on campaign. The battles are few and far between, but the rain and mosquitoes never stop. Nor do the card games, the complaints about the food, the—er—" Now how could he phrase this politely? "The stories."

"Stories? You mean gossip?" She sounded amused. "I've never before heard a gentleman admit that men gossip."

"Perhaps one just becomes more truthful in the army. Deathbed confessions, and all that."

"Of course." Her smile was knowing, and he realized that she understood his dry humor. He'd been so often misunderstood in the past, but Atalanta and he just seemed to think alike.

He'd felt it all along, in fact. "Things are so different here," he said. She looked like she would understand what no one else had except other veterans. "In the army, you know you may die any day. And you know that any of the men around you may, too."

"Of course, that's true for us at home, too."

When her father died, she must have learned that the hard way. "Yes, it is, of course," he said. "Perhaps in the military the difference is that we don't deny the truth. Death doesn't arrive unexpectedly for us—we're always waiting for it."

But that didn't sound quite right. "I don't mean to make it sound like we're all fatalistic out there—far from it. But it's hard to ignore death when you're in the middle of it."

Or when you cause it. "There were many times I thought the end had come for me. Once a mortar shell exploded next to me, and Folly panicked and ran. And I—who always prided myself on my seat—went headfirst onto a rock. I thought that was the end—well, until I hit the rock. Then I didn't think much of anything for a while."

"Was Icarus—was Folly hurt?"

He should remember to use her names for the horses. "When I came to, Icarus was fine. It's hard to train a horse to ignore loud noises."

"I can imagine."

The road in front of them widened, and the traffic increased. He saw that they were coming to Park Lane, but north of Hyde Park Corner and busy Rotten Row. "Shall we walk in the Park?" he said. "I believe this area is quieter, and we're not likely to be spied by anyone but children and their nursemaids."

She paused, gazing across the busy road at the green expanse of the Park. "That would be nice," she finally said. "I do miss the country."

"So do I. Nothing is stuffier or dustier than London, somehow." He led her to the curb and watched for an opportunity to cross. "Don't get me wrong, Miss James—I am very fond of London. But it isn't—" He broke off. He'd been about to say "where my heart lies," but that was just too personal. "It isn't where I'd most like to be," he finished lamely.

When the coaches and wagons cleared, he helped her across the wide street. They strolled down the walkway to a high arched gate. He held the gate open for her, and they entered the airy woodland.

They walked under the shady trees for a bit. The daffodils were out, yellow and white, standing in cheerful clumps amid the grass and undergrowth.

"Here's a bench," he said, checking first that it was clean and dry. "Would you like to sit for a bit?"

"Certainly." As she sat, she arranged her skirts about her with a careful hand. He supposed if a lady didn't have many articles of clothing, she had to be mindful of those she had.

There was so much he had never considered. And it seemed to be the same for her. Their worlds were so different, despite the fact that she had always seemed oddly familiar to him. Comfortable.

Well, not comfortable, exactly. He was usually intrigued or angry, worried or frustrated around her. It came of concern for her, he supposed.

But he hardly knew her. He couldn't really feel for her, of course. It was just an illusion brought about by how much she was in his thoughts.

Not that that made any sense.

He sat beside her on the bench and leaned against the cold iron back. He stared up at the leaves, the branches, the sky, and thought how different England looked from Spain or Portugal.

He glanced at her face. She wore the brim of her bonnet low, shadowing much of her expression, but he could still see the blotches that weeping had caused.

He'd done that to her. "Miss James," he said, deciding to give it a second try. "I don't expect this will carry much weight with you, but your horses were invaluable to us in the Peninsula. Particularly Minerva."

She had been an elegant horse, just as Atalanta had claimed. "Basty was shorter and lighter than I, so I rode

Icarus, and he Minerva. There was one battle in Spain, at Talavera . . ."

It had been a while since he'd brought all that day's details to mind—soldiers learned early on not to dwell on losses. And near-losses were as bad—you could forever try to find meaning in what happened. Why did I live? Why did he die? It dragged a man down, made a bad soldier of him.

But strangely enough, the memories were perfectly clear. "We were in the middle of a charge, but something had gone wrong. I think the scouts had been misled as to the enemy's strength. Hard to tell."

He paused, seeing the smoke and mud all about. "Their artillery had taken a hard toll on us—we didn't realize how much until after it was all over. But it was obvious that we were disorganized. Sebastian was to my right, on Minerva. We hit the French cavalry hard."

He shook his head. "It's impossible to describe what it's like, being in the middle of a battle. You can rarely see more than what's right in front of you. You have a saber slashing down at you, and if you're lucky, you get there first, or deflect it. Then you strike back, fast. If you succeed, there's already another horse upon you, another saber, or occasionally a pistol pointed at your chest."

He stared up into the peaceful trees. "All you can hear is the shouting at a charge, the guns, the artillery. The screaming. And there's smoke all over. It gets in your nose, in your eyes. Dirt, mud. Blood. Horses falling all around."

But this wasn't what he'd meant to say. "On top of everything, it was foggy that day. It looked like the plains of hell. Out of nowhere came a French dragoon, his sword covered with blood. He slashed Sebastian before I could shout a warning."

She gave a distressed cry. "Was he all right?"

He rubbed at the tension in his forehead. "A saber in the face is never a pretty sight. God knows, we disfigured plenty of French, so it was no surprise. But he was all right, yes. Thanks to Minerva."

He noticed her hands were clenched in her lap. "Really? She helped him?"

"She saved his life. I thought he was dead, honest to God—or at least unconscious. He told me later he was dazed, but aware of everything that happened. He couldn't see anything for all the blood, and he had to struggle to breathe. He was certain he was a goner. I saw him slump forward over his horse's neck, and I tried to get over to him. But those damned frogs just kept coming."

What was wrong with him? He shouldn't be swearing in front of a lady.

He forced himself to take a deep, slow breath. "I beg your pardon, Miss James. I shouldn't get carried away like that."

She shook her head quickly. "You have nothing to apologize for. I know how hard it is to talk about some things."

They'd both seen tragedy, that was for sure. "What I meant to say was, I was surrounded. It was all I could do to stay alive myself, and I thought it was all up for poor Basty. But somehow that blessed horse got him out of it."

"She did?" Her voice sounded proud.

"That's right. With a dead weight on her, and surrounded by cavalry on all sides, she managed to keep Basty on her back and get him behind the lines. A lesser horse would have panicked. Dash it, practically any horse would have panicked—you know that. No guidance, reins trailing, explosions on all sides . . ."

He shook his head in wonder. "By the time the battle was over, I went looking for him, figuring it was too late to do anything but bury him. And there he was, being mauled by our drunken physician. I'll tell you this much, I was never so glad to see Basty's ugly face as I was at that instant."

She moved her hand, as if to pat his, but pulled it back immediately. "Was he badly scarred?"

He shrugged. "Well, he lived. That was the important part. He was afraid his Charlotte wouldn't want him any more, but I know she would have had him in any condition she could."

"You knew her?"

It was all so difficult. "No. I didn't meet her until—until I sold out. I'd written her the letter when he, ah . . . when he didn't make it at Albuera. But a letter is so cold. A piece of paper, and a little ink. That sort of news deserves something more. He deserved more."

"So you called on her when you got home?"

"That's right. Pretty little thing, she was, too. She'd known he was scarred, but she'd written him the warmest letter, saying how little that mattered to her." He smiled at the memory. "And that's what we'd all been telling him. Why, any girl who'd have wanted his ugly mug in the first place wouldn't mind a little scratch on it. Hell, some of us thought he looked better after then he had before."

She stirred uncomfortably. Dash it, he'd done it again. "I suppose it sounds harsh, but that's the sort of thing that keeps a man alive through such things—laughter."

She nodded. "I understand, believe me. Tom and I have had our share of dark jokes. You should hear what he calls his—er, no, never mind."

It sounded interesting, actually, but he didn't want to embarrass her by pressing the point.

She gave a small sigh. That wasn't a good sign. "What's the matter?" he asked gently.

She gazed up at him, her eyes sad. "It sounds like a story in a book, for a while. A fairy tale, perhaps—the sort with an inspiring moral. He's disfigured, and fears his sweetheart won't want him any more. But it turns out her love is stronger than he thought. Except that—"

So she understood what he was saying. "Except that the

story isn't supposed to end with him dying before he can see her again, is it? It makes you wonder what the whole point is."

He shook his head. "That's something you're always struggling with at such times. The randomness. The apparent lack of rhyme or reason."

She nodded. "One tends to look for meaning where meaning doesn't exist. It's comforting to imagine we live in a perfectly neat world, one without random chance."

"Exactly," he said firmly. "That's what bothers me about high-stakes gaming. The players may think they're playing the odds, but they aren't. Even when there isn't a house to take all the money, the punters get carried away with imagined streaks of luck, and hunches, and feelings. They should look at the numbers, not their emotions."

"That's so true," she said, giving him an earnest look. "My father knew the odds—why, he made tables and charts based on Laplace's calculus of probability. Did you know the commonly believed odds for hazard are incorrect?"

"Really?"

She nodded with great certainty. "Oh, yes. If you just do the mathematics, you'll see that—" She broke off suddenly. "Oh dear, I must be sending you to sleep."

So she knew maths and probabilities? She was endlessly intriguing.

But . . . wait. He sat back against the hard iron, puzzled. She might know a lot of theory, but she didn't apply her knowledge very well, did she? He'd seen her play piquet. Perhaps she became nervous? Or did she only imperfectly understand her father's calculations?

She carefully brushed back a stray curl which had escaped her coiled braids. "What I meant to say was that my father knew all the odds, perfectly. But when the cards were in his hand, he somehow became convinced that he could feel his luck. Winning streaks, losing streaks—my fortune's about to turn, I can feel it. Yes, I've heard it all. And it's frustrating, isn't it, to not be able to talk sense into someone in that position?"

She was a mystery, that was for certain. So why did she persist in playing cards?

She adjusted her bonnet, then clasped her hands in her lap again. "Could you tell me what happened to Minerva? And Icarus, too, of course."

These weren't things he particularly liked to remember. "Icarus died early in '11—January, I think it was. Cold as a witch's—er—dashed cold, it was." He really had to stop using rough language. He wasn't in the field any longer. "We were in formation, prepared to advance. There was a barrage of artillery, and the next thing I knew, there was a mortar shell exploding right in front of me. Icarus took most of the blast. I never had a better horse, I can tell you that."

She sat there saying nothing, her face somber. Why did these things never get any easier?

She swallowed. "And Minerva?"

That had been a hellish day. The worst action he'd ever been in, and the most frustrating. "The battle was in the hills near Albuera. Everything was confusion—the rain, the mud the horses kicked up. That was a terrible sight."

He didn't want to remember, but he owed her that much. "We didn't have enough cavalry, not by a long sight. The cavalry are there to protect the infantry—but we couldn't. We didn't." He sighed. "The infantry didn't have time to get into proper formation. There was a terrible slaughter when the French cavalry got through."

He leaned back and stared at the sky of England, the sky he never thought he'd see again. "Sebastian was wounded in the leg—I didn't realize how badly. He'd deflected a saber thrust, but the point had entered his thigh. I told him to go behind the lines, to find a surgeon." He rubbed his eyes. "I should have insisted."

She laid her hand on his arm. "You did the best anyone could, I am certain."

She was right. It was no good blaming himself for it. "In any case, I didn't insist. We were in the middle of a battle, after all—you only have seconds to say anything, or even think. And God knows, cavalrymen spend little enough time thinking. Wellington cursed us many times, did you know that?"

She looked surprised. "He cursed you?"

"Well, not me personally," he said, enjoying the image of the Iron Duke dressing down the future Earl of Stoke. "I mean he cursed the cavalry. The men get carried away, you see, and they forget all sense. Seem to think they're at a fox hunt or something. Stupid."

He leaned forward, his hands on his knees. "So there we were, in the middle of the battle. I was having a hard time of it—I no longer had Icarus, and my new mount spooked at everything. Not what you want in a cavalry horse, let me tell you."

He could almost taste the blood in his mouth. "A troop of French dragoons were heading right for us, and my damned horse wouldn't turn. There's nothing more vulnerable than a cavalryman on a bad horse, believe me. I could have gotten off and run for it, but then it would have been child's play for anyone behind me to swipe my head off. So I was stuck there, swearing at my useless horse and convinced those were my last moments on earth."

He took a deep breath. "Next thing I knew, there was Basty, being a damned idiot as usual. Thought he had to rescue me for some reason. Not worth it, I can tell you—but that's what he wanted."

He stared down at the ground, the images coming fast. "He was on Minerva. He rode her between me and the on-coming charge, figuring Minerva's presence might calm my stupid mount, and he could get us out of there." He'd called him a fool. He'd wished many times those hadn't been his last words to Basty. "He planned to save me. But there wasn't time."

He rubbed his jaw, determined to get through this. "The front dragoon slashed at him, but Minerva reared, kicked out with her front hooves. She got the dragoon in the head, but not before he'd slashed her neck."

Atalanta's head was down and her bonnet hid her face entirely, but he thought he could hear a quiet sob. "She went down fast. And Basty—his leg was no good after that wound. Couldn't get his leg out of the stirrup in time." He let out a shaky breath. "At least he died quickly."

They sat there in silence for a long while, the trees whispering in the breeze. The sounds of children playing near the Serpentine wafted over to them—laughter, shouting.

All about them was life. "What I came to tell you," he said slowly, "was that Minerva saved my life, and once saved his. And believe me, his life was worth saving."

His eyes stung, but he was too proud to brush at them and betray himself. So he stared intently at the clouds and tried to regain control.

He felt a soft touch, and looked down. With some hesitation, she slipped her small hand into his.

It was strangely comforting, sitting here with her hand in his. Knowing that she understood his sorrow, and he understood hers. He didn't know why it should be so, but it was.

And as they sat there under the canopy of leaves, he felt like he was finally home.

Atalanta stared at her one good evening gown. After all that had happened today, she felt strangely reluctant to put on the aqua silk and become a card player again. Her day in the Park had reminded her of what she'd once wanted her life to be—full of life and beauty, friendship and . . . and love.

Not that she was in love with the Earl of Stoke. Why, his name still gave her a chill whenever she heard it. But to be honest, he'd fixed himself in her mind, her world. If her life had continued to be as happy and sheltered as once seemed inevitable, perhaps she would have ended up with a man like Stoke. She could have brought sunshine to his life, and warmth. She would have had the time and strength to carry his burdens.

Now it was all she could do to carry hers.

She adjusted her stockings and turned to her gown. It only took a moment to don it and fix the front ties. She shook out its silk skirt and looked into the dull pier glass. She would do, though if her color stayed so white, her companions would be fetching the smelling salts.

She didn't know how one's outlook on life could change so much, so rapidly—and yet change nothing. While she'd been mourning Minerva and Icarus, and comforting Tom in their loss, the horses had been fighting in the wars. She remembered back when they all lived in daily fear of the dreaded Bonaparte invading England.

Now, because of men like Lord Stoke, they were safe from invasion. In a few years' time, Spain too might be free from the bloody ravages of the French troops.

Surely that was worth the life of a horse. Even Minerva.

She felt small now, petty. Stoke had risked his life, and his friends had died, all for a cause outside themselves. And she'd been consumed only with things happening in England. No, not even England—just her family, her little life. Somehow, she'd never realized how large the world was, how varied. And what a small thing she and her problems were.

Of course, even an officer like Stoke was only a tiny part of the British army, and the British army was only one of many fighting to stop France's bid to conquer all of Europe. So in a way, their situations were similar. He had his duties, and she had hers. Though caring for Tom and Louly might not rank with a soldier's duty, it was her own. And though taking the tarnish off her family name might not rate with defending Britain, her father's tragedy deserved redress.

She would see it through. She no longer bore any ill will toward Lord Stoke, even though his family had been dining off the ruin of the James family for years. Even though he'd taken her gentle Minerva into war to be slaughtered like a piece of meat. But she knew her duty. And if Stoke stood in her way, he would be her enemy.

No matter how she felt about him personally.

Chapter Eight

S toke strode up the crimson-carpeted staircase in Lady Isabella's opulent townhouse and wondered what he was doing here. Surely Miss James wouldn't attend, not after what she'd said this afternoon about the fallacy of luck.

So though he'd promised her a game of piquet yesterday, that had been before this afternoon's . . . conversation. Or whatever it had been. He felt like he knew her better than he had ever known any woman. He'd shared things with her he'd never expected to.

But he was a man of his word. So just in case she'd come to try her hand again at cards, he would be here first. If she wanted to play, let her play with him.

That should keep her away from Malkham and his ilk.

He entered the gaming room slowly, assessing the territory first. There were fewer punters here than last week, but that might be because the night was young yet. The infernal macao table was already surrounded by a group of young bucks, but the rest of the room was fairly quiet.

He seemed to have arrived before Miss James—if she was even coming. He glanced about, wondering if he should amuse himself with a glass of wine while pretending not to wait, when he felt her presence.

He turned his head sharply, and yes, there she was. What

was it about her that made it possible for him to feel her energy across the room?

She'd been in the other card room, he saw, the one devoted to loo and commerce and the like. She was in the same gown she'd worn the first night he saw her—in fact, it looked like nothing at all had changed about her. Her coronet of braids was still the golden hue of dark honey, and she stood still and white like a statue. A statue of the mythical Greek heroine she was named for—or perhaps the name Edmund had called her, the Goddess of the Cards.

He felt faintly disturbed. Not just that she was here at all, but—what was it? Perhaps the way she looked totally unchanged. As if their confidences earlier had meant nothing, had affected her not at all.

He didn't feel one whit the same. How could she? Was it all deception?

And if so, which Atalanta was the real one?

Her eyes flicked up and met his, and they were calm, collected. She'd known he was there, hadn't she?

He crossed the burgundy carpet to where she stood. "Good evening, Miss James." He felt like he was playing a part, pretending to barely know her. He didn't like the feeling.

"Good evening, Lord Stoke," she said serenely. "I don't suppose you would care for a game of piquet?"

He tried to appear nonchalant. "Not particularly, I confess. Would you care to try your hand at loo?"

She raised an eyebrow. "I'm disappointed in you, Stoke. Loo, indeed. Are you afraid that you'll lose to me again?"

What was she playing at? Her voice was distant, controlled, as if she were acting a part as well. He felt as if they were puppets in a drama he knew nothing of, and some mysterious person was pushing him into a situation he didn't like.

And perhaps that person was Atalanta. "Do you never tire

of piquet, Miss James? I thought a person of your acumen would see the futility of wagering on chance."

A cool smile touched her lips. "Oh, but I don't intend to wager on chance, Lord Stoke. I mean to wager on skill. My skill. Are you up to the challenge?"

Hang the girl. "You are determined to play?"

She tilted her head to one side, and the end of a blue satin ribbon slipped loose from her coil of braids. "I am. Piquet is my passion, you must know. And if you do not care to be my partner, I am sure there are many men who would be eager to try their luck with me."

She glanced around the room deliberately. "Have you seen Lord Malkham here, by any chance?"

She was playing a game with him, but he didn't know its purpose. If he left her to the mercies of the scoundrel Malkham, it would serve her right. He'd done all he could to warn her off him. Why was she so set on destruction? She knew enough not to trust to fickle fortune.

Or was that it? He could see the tension in every part of her, from the tightness in her smooth neck, down to the nervous tapping of her delicate foot. She didn't look like a woman in the grip of the cards.

No, she looked like a woman who was planning something. And planning was something that most punters never did.

"Do you trust your skill so much?" he asked, wondering what her reaction would be.

Her smile was mysterious. "I do."

It would be her ruin, too. An experienced player with a head more for statistics than luck could count on coming out the winner more times than not in piquet. But from her play last week, he knew her to be no match for Malkham, or for most serious piquet players.

Perhaps when she had beaten him last time, it had increased her confidence. He didn't want to see her lose what she didn't have, but still less did he want to be part of the cause.

If he played her now, he could show her how imperfect her technique was, before she had the opportunity of playing a man who would not be looking out for her interests.

"Very well," he said with a nod. "I would be pleased if you would favor me with a game of piquet, Miss James. A rematch, if you will."

She smiled, but it looked more like triumph than happiness.

He led her to a quiet table by the tall sash windows, and they cut for deal. When she won the first deal, he said, "Do you wish me to shuffle for you again?"

"Of course." Perhaps she saw the disapproval in his eyes, for she gave him a bland look. "I trust you."

"At least cut the pack afterwards," he said. He picked up the cards and began to shuffle. "It's not a good habit to get into, you know. Oh, it's common among social games, but if you play piquet with serious card players, you should be up to all the rigs."

She pursed her lips. "Are you saying you're going to fleece me?"

His breath came out in a snort. "Of course I'm not, and you know it. I'm just saying that others might not be so punctilious."

She examined her smooth fingernails, and he realized her hands were without gloves so she could better hold the cards. "Are you saying people cheat?"

"Hush." He glanced around the room. "That is not a word you should ever say in a place like this. Admittedly, no one is likely to call you out for it, but they might call me out as your companion."

"My companion?"

"I mean your—your opponent."

"Very well then." She lay her hand down on the green

baize. "Are you saying that people actually do that dishonorable thing that you won't let me name?"

She was incorrigible. "It's been known to happen. It's probably the worst crime a gentleman can be accused of, but some suspect that sharpsters are not only to be found in the squalid gaming hells off St. James's Street." He handed the pack to her. "Here, cut."

She did, then pushed the pack back toward him. "You should cut now, right?" Her smile was pert. "When you've done teaching me the etiquette of gaming, perhaps I can teach you my winning strategies."

She hadn't won last time through skill, only random chance. "And perhaps I can teach you mine."

She continued smiling, but her eyes were on the cards. "Agreed. Shall we play for guinea points, then, to make it more interesting?"

"Guinea points?" Was the girl mad? "You don't have that sort of money to lose."

She raised her eyebrows.

Drat his quick tongue. "What I mean to say is, I don't expect you do, and neither do I."

She gave him a disbelieving look. "The Earl of Stoke, one of the wealthiest men in England, doesn't have a few measly guineas?"

It was devilishly hard to protect someone who fought your help at every turn. "Let me put it this way, Miss James. I don't play cards with people who cannot afford to lose." She of all people should respect this. "You said yourself that it was morally inexcusable to play against such a person, did you not?"

She clasped her hands together as though she was nervous, but her smile was perfectly collected. "Oh, I see what you mean. But you misunderstand me. I have the money right here, ready and eager to be lost."

She opened her drawstring reticule and showed him a

pile of gold coins. "Of course," she continued, "I don't expect to lose."

Who did? She had him at *point non plus*, and she knew it. And if she was determined to play piquet at such heady stakes, better with him than with Malkham. He would try to only beat her by a few points—just enough to teach her she was not the player she thought she was. And if his luck went against him and he won a large sum, surely he would be able to find a way to pay it back to her.

"Agreed, then," he said, cutting the pack. "Now do put those away, before we have a flock of vultures coming down on us."

"Do vultures really flock?" she asked, closing up her bag. "It sounds remarkably domestic." She took up the cards and began to deal. "Oh, by the way, I forgot to ask," she said, smiling wickedly up at him. "Did you remember to bring money this time?"

"Yes. Though I don't expect to lose," he said meaningfully.

She pursed her lips. "No one ever does."

He felt an odd sensation run across his skin as she echoed his earlier thoughts. How could she seem so familiar to him in her every word, so much a part of him, and yet be so completely a mystery?

She finished dealing the cards, and set the remainder down with a crisp snap.

He arranged his cards, then waited while she finished sorting hers. She was slow in making her discards, too, wrinkling her forehead and biting the inside of her cheek while she decided. Finally, she took up only three of the four cards remaining.

She might still do well, of course. "Point of four," he said.

She studied her cards, frowning slightly in concentration. "Good."

That made it easy. She must have three cards of each suit. "Run of four to the queen—good, of course. And three kings."

She checked her cards. "Good."

She was so transparent. Had her father been such a poor teacher? Or just a poor player? From the moment she picked up her discards, she should know almost to a card what he had. And she shouldn't have to check to see if she had three aces.

He led the ace of diamonds, and play went slowly for several tricks. But when he led the queen of clubs, she reached for a card and paused.

"Oh dear," she said. She pulled a card out of the right side of her hand and put it in toward the left.

So—she was mixing up her clubs and spades? She needed someone watching her day and night. And he could tell exactly what card it was, too—she kept her hand in perfect order, so he could always tell what card she was about to play.

Her mistake threw off his strategy, though, because it meant her queen of spades was protected after all. By the end of the hand, he was surprised to find she had taken more tricks than he had.

When she finished counting up her cards, she pushed them across the table to him. "Will you shuffle again for me?"

"It's my deal."

She shrugged, smiling at her error. "I always lose count. Sorry."

"Don't think anything of it." He shuffled the cards, reminded her to cut, and dealt out the hand. She dithered a long time over her discards, meaning she was either throwing high cards, or breaking up a long suit. Finally, she discarded the maximum number of cards, and wrinkled her nose when she saw what she got for them.

When he exchanged his discards for the remaining three cards, he realized she must have thrown some of her best cards away. His hand was terrible, so if she was disappointed with hers, she must have judged her chances badly.

Or played a hunch. Well, perhaps this would teach her to practice what she preached. "Always play the odds" was his philosophy, in cards as well as in battle.

One of Lady Isabella's bewigged footmen approached the table. "Would either of you like some refreshment? Glass of wine, some biscuits?"

"Oh," said Atalanta, putting her cards down distractedly. "I left my glass in the other room, on the table with the green jade thingummy on it. Could you possible get it for me?"

If she'd been drinking, that explained a lot. Perhaps he should go easier on her. He didn't want her to lose too much.

She stared at her cards, touching each one as if she was counting them. "Point of five," she said finally.

"Good."

She gave a delighted smile, as if she were a little girl given a present. "Sequence of five," she declared proudly. "That is, er . . . quint."

He hadn't expected that. So her cards were better than she'd at first thought. Well, that wasn't unusual. A sequence of low cards didn't always jump out at one.

She frowned, as if trying to remember something. "Sequence of five—that's fifteen points, right? I always forget where it jumps up, at five or six."

"You're correct. Fifteen points."

She smiled, and her smile became even brighter when the footman brought her a crystal glass half-full of claret. She frowned at her cards again. "Three of a kind."

She had three aces, of course. "Good." That meant she was at twenty-three points for the hand. He'd have to take care she didn't reach thirty points and get a pique—that would bring her a bonus of thirty points, which might be enough to throw the whole game in her favor. It would be unfortunate if another lucky chance led her to challenge Malkham.

"Oh, that's wonderful," she said. She squinted at her cards. "That wasn't enough to repique you, was it?"

"You're at twenty-three for the hand. You would need to have reached thirty before you lead a card in play to have a repique."

She wrinkled her nose at him. "I know that. I told you I know how to play. I just lose count." She casually picked up her wine glass and took a drink. "I suppose I shall just have to pique you then. Or capot you." She grinned like the cat that ate the canary, and held up her glass as if toasting him. "Or both."

"We shall see."

She reached for a card, then paused. "Five guineas says I get both a pique and a capot."

How much had she drunk? Or, still worse, was it that the fever of the cards had taken hold of her? "That's ridiculous," he said.

She pouted. "One guinea?"

He rolled his eyes. "An uneven wager like that gets uneven odds." She was the most gullible pigeon he'd ever seen, ripe for plucking. "Very well. If you must, I'll give you ten guineas at a hundred to one that you don't."

She looked blank. "That would be shillings and pence," she said after a moment. "I hate dividing shillings and pence. Why don't we make it a hundred guineas to me if I pique and capot you, and one guinea to you if I don't?"

"Very well." Even at those odds, it was a bad bargain for her. Why, he had ace, king, and queen of clubs, and a protected king of diamonds. She didn't stand a chance of a capot.

She lay down the ace of hearts. He saw that she had four

spades to the left of it, so that would be the ace down to the knave.

He played his singleton queen of hearts, and sat back to see how long her hearts suit was. She played her cards in strict order as always, down to the nine.

Wait a minute.

He examined his cards again. This didn't make sense. If she didn't have the seven or eight, where the hell was her sequence of five?

Then again, if she did have the seven and eight, why had she declared point of five when she could have declared point of seven?

She bit her lip and studied her cards. After a moment, she brought out the eight of hearts.

So they were there. "You declared a point of five," he said, throwing his eight of diamonds on her heart.

She squinted at his cards, as if she had trouble telling diamonds from hearts. Finally, she took the trick, and led out her seven. "What did you say?"

He threw a low spade. "You declared a point of five, but you had a point of seven."

She frowned as she scooped up the trick. "But I only had five in a row."

Oh, for heaven's sake. "That's sequence, not point. Point doesn't have to be in sequence. Hence the name."

She gave him an embarrassed smile. "I knew that." She played the ace of diamonds, then moved on to spades.

It was exactly what he'd calculated. The rest of her cards were spades, so he needed to protect his queen of spades or she'd get her blessed capot.

He paused for a second. She'd piqued him, hadn't she? It had gone by without his noticing. Good lord, but his cards were bad. That seven-card suit of hers had changed everything.

Well, at least he could stop her capot, though she'd still be a fair number of points ahead of him.

The play went as he expected for the next several tricks. When she led the final card, he produced his queen and picked up the trick.

"That's mine, I think." Her voice was polite, but firm.

"My queen takes it," he explained.

"But I led diamonds."

She . . . what? He turned over the cards, and the queen of diamonds stared him in the face.

Blast. "Where'd you get that queen?"

Her expression was blank. "I always had it."

"But you—you always—" Hell. She'd capotted him after all. How likely was that?

She must have drunk more than he'd realized. Perhaps she'd sipped several glasses before he'd arrived. Her play was certainly clumsy.

She grinned at him. "I think you owe me a hundred guineas."

"I owe you a lot more than that." He did a quick calculation. "That finishes the game." That had been fast.

"The game's over? Did I get a hundred points already?"

"More than that. Let's see. . . . Forty for the capot, thirty for the pique, twenty-three, plus thirteen. That's a hundred and six points, plus seventeen from the last hand."

"A hundred and twenty-three points?" She gaped at him. "That means—"

This whole thing felt unreal. "As I got fourteen points, you win a hundred and nine guineas." He felt like he needed a glass of wine himself. "Plus a hundred guineas."

She gave him a delighted smile. "I told you I would pique you. And capot you." She sat back in her chair and tilted her head to one side. "But I had no idea it would be so much fun."

Chapter Nine

*T*hings were going well so far. Over two hundred
guineas! She hadn't expected to win nearly as much
from Lord Stoke. Fifty, perhaps, and after quite a few more
hands than two.

That had been a real stroke of luck. Not that she believed
in luck.

Now for Malkham. Tom's information had said that, somehow, Malkham was running out of funds again. She had no
idea how one man could run through so much money in only
five years, but he seemed to have run through much of what
he'd won from her father.

Lost it at cards, perhaps, or at hazard. Did he have the
thirst to always play? She couldn't tell. She could hardly tell
anything at all from him. He was impossible to read.

Not like Lord Stoke. Stoke's emotions were all too clear
to her, though she didn't expect he realized it. Perhaps it was
because he was so like her, and she recognized what was
going through his mind.

Or perhaps it was because the strength of his emotions re-
sisted his efforts to keep them in check.

She'd enjoyed winning that money from him. His protective instincts made her feel warm and cared for, and she

truly respected him for them. But he was a little too quick to believe that she was totally incompetent.

It had been fun to disabuse him of the notion.

Or had she? Had her ruse been so good that he still believed her to be an idiot? Didn't he see that she was behaving quite differently than she had this afternoon?

Perhaps the wine had done the trick.

She gazed around Lady Isabella's overheated drawing room and sighed. She would much rather be outside. Anywhere but here, in fact. But she had more to do.

After her win, she'd gone into the other room, and was now in the middle of a game of cassino with a middle-aged lady who had brightly rouged cheeks. For all her protestations, Atalanta did enjoy cards. She just didn't care much for the betting aspect of it.

Though she had felt a thrill at winning such a large amount from Stoke. Perhaps if she hadn't learned her lesson at such a young age, she would have become an inveterate gamester herself.

She enjoyed cassino, with its quick pace and relaxingly simple strategy. They were playing for shilling points, of course, which was a relief to her after the last game.

If she'd lost to Stoke, after all, her whole plan might have been thrown off. Of course, she would have tried to talk him into a rematch, hoping that eventually her skill together with his misconceptions would make her the winner.

Thank goodness it had all gone right.

Now she was on the lookout for Lord Malkham. She should be able to detect him by his smell. The smell of a rat.

How could he go on in society and have everyone think well of him? How could they not have spied out his true character long ago?

These reflections absorbed her until she caught a glimpse of her prey through the stately double doors to the other gaming room. Malkham.

He wasn't likely to leave soon, so she took her time over her current game. No point in alerting anyone that anything was out of the ordinary.

Finally her opponent swept up the last cards. "I believe you now owe me four shillings, Miss James."

She smiled at the powdery lady and paid the small sum. "Thank you for the game. I enjoyed it."

"As did I."

Atalanta gathered up her reticule, now containing several large bank notes from Stoke in addition to the coins that she had started with, and her half-empty wine glass. She hoped no one noticed that she was still on her first glass of wine. Hopefully the footman wouldn't say anything to Malkham to put him on his guard.

She walked slowly and gracefully into the next room, the pristine Goddess of the Cards casually looking for another game.

Yes, there was Malkham, leaning over the macao table. She had to draw him away quickly, for if he became entangled in a game there, he might not rise from the table for hours. Macao players were always persistent in their desire to lose large sums of money.

She strolled up to his right arm. "Lord Malkham?" she said. "Good evening to you once again."

His glittering eyes surveyed her. "So it's the James chit again, is it? Here to win still more from an elderly man?"

She gave him a brief smile. "My intention precisely. Are you in the mood for piquet?"

His dry lips tightened into a cold smile. "I am always in the mood for the cards, girl. You would know that if you knew anything about me."

She tried to look smug. "I won a tidy sum earlier this evening. Would you care to raise the stakes?"

She noticed a glint in his bloodshot eyes. "If that's your preference. Shall we?"

He extended his arm to lead her to the table in the corner, the same one they had played at the previous week.

She didn't want to touch him. She didn't think she could, in fact. As important as her ruse was to her, she still couldn't bring herself to be that close to him, hating him as she did.

So she pretended not to notice his proffered arm. "Shall we play for guinea points?" she said, making her own way to the table.

"Guinea points?" It was hard to tell what he was thinking, but his voice was slow, pointed.

She gave him a nonchalant smile as one of the everpresent footmen pulled out a chair for her. "Lord Stoke was willing to play me for guinea points. And I won, too."

He narrowed his gaze. "You don't say? Distracted, I expect."

She would show him. By the end of the night, he would regret that he ever doubted her acumen. And regret that he had ever heard her name.

She gave him her most innocent smile. "Shall we cut for deal?"

Stoke didn't know what to think. Had he been distracted by the scent of her, that faint perfume of violets, mixed with the tang of her skin, her hair?

How else could he account for losing to her, and by so much?

He tried to review the game, but the details seemed fuzzy now. Why had he been so certain of what cards she held?

And how would he explain this to Edmund? Oh, he could hide it of course, but he detested lies and pretense. So what would he say? After lecturing you about your wagering, I lost over two hundred guineas on one hand?

So he'd meant to teach her a lesson? Seems she'd taught him a lesson—a lesson about how random chance meant exactly that. Not certainty. Chance.

His impulse was to leave now, to go home and brood over Miss Atalanta James in the privacy of his library. Oh, he wouldn't mean to, but that's exactly what he'd be doing. That seemed to be all he'd been doing ever since he met her.

What was her hold over him?

He tried to distract himself with a game of speculation, but his mind was on other things, and he lost again. Only a small sum, thankfully, but it was a loss just the same. One more sin to chalk up to his self-righteousness, he supposed.

He was just wondering what to do next when he saw Malkham stroll in.

No. Not Malkham. She wouldn't play with him, would she? Surely she could be satisfied with winning over two hundred guineas, without trying for more.

But perhaps her win had given her confidence . . . confidence she shouldn't have.

Perhaps she would now lose everything she had to Malkham, and it would be all Stoke's fault. He might try to give her money, make up the loss, but she wouldn't take it, would she? She couldn't. If a lady took money from a gentleman, it meant one thing only—that she was his mistress. And Atalanta would never do anything of the kind.

So why did the idea tantalize him so? Why did it linger in his mind, get into his skin?

This was ridiculous. If he wanted the girl so much, he should just marry her. She was a viscount's daughter, for God's sake. She wasn't someone who would become anyone's mistress.

But he couldn't marry her. He knew that. Even if she hadn't been a dedicated gamester, it would still be out of the question. Which was probably why the thought hadn't occurred to him before, given his near-obsession with her.

He had his duties to think of. His family, his dependents, his tenants. His future children. And to give them what they deserved, what the name of Stoke deserved, what his line deserved, he needed to marry a woman of fortune and connections, as well as breeding.

She had the breeding, of course. There were few more highly born females in the country. But she had no money to speak of—not counting the two hundred guineas she'd just won off him. And she had no worthwhile connections. Her close relatives despised her, and they clearly lacked wealth and connections themselves. If there had been anyone else in her life who could help her, they would have done so long before now.

Long before she turned to the cards.

There she was, just as he'd feared. Her head held high, she approached Malkham and had a brief conversation with him. They seemed to agree on something.

Damn. He saw Malkham offer his arm to Atalanta, and he thought he caught a brief glimpse of revulsion in her eyes before her expression went bland.

She followed Malkham to a table in the corner, and they prepared to play a game of piquet.

Several occupants of the room noticed, too. He could see the heads turn, the whispers, the interest. Was it just interest in the Goddess of the Cards? Or was there something else going on?

And why were several of the whisperers looking at him? Oh, hell. They all knew about that game, didn't they? The game in which Atalanta's father had lost his fortune to Malkham, Sir Geoffrey Yarrow, and his own father. He hadn't realized it was common knowledge.

A group of macao players abandoned their table to watch the piquet game. Stoke knew this would be frowned on at real gaming hells, where cheating was always a danger, but he supposed at a *ton* party like this, such doings were acceptable. After all, if a player was worried about people seeing his cards and signaling them to his opponent, he could just keep them close to his chest.

Malkham noticed the lookers-on as well, and a bitter smile stretched his thin lips. Did he prefer to fleece the lambs with an audience to gawk?

Stoke didn't think he could stand to watch this. It was like a scene of carnage—horrible to see, but impossible to turn away from. But he had to know what would happen. If she needed help, he would be here for her.

He rose from his chair and tried not to look interested as he made his way across to the table where Atalanta and Malkham sat. Her back was straight and her position serene, as if she knew everything that was going to happen.

He studied her face—what he could see from where he stood. Her cheeks were more flushed now than they had been. She no longer looked ready to faint.

Was it the wine? He felt a surge of irritation. If she were his, he'd do something about that. And something about her gaming, too.

The play went calmly on, though he found himself watching Atalanta's delicate jawline more than the cards. The first hand was without much interest, Malkham moving ahead by a few points.

But for some reason, none of the spectators lost interest. On the contrary, more gathered around them—so many that he was afraid if he didn't take care, he would no longer be able to see the game.

He moved to his right a bit, and had a clear view once again, though from behind her, so he could no longer see her face.

Someone in front of him jostled her a bit, and for a fraction of a second he could see her cards.

Well, he'd be damned. His glimpse hadn't been enough to see exactly what she held, but he had clearly seen red cards mixed in with her spades.

She couldn't be . . . No, that would be ridiculous. It had to be the wine.

Didn't it?

More intrigued than ever, he started paying closer attention to the proceedings. Now that his suspicions were roused, things began to make sense.

He circled around the group, until he was closer to Malkham than to his intriguing lady. From here he could see every card played, as well as every hesitation of the fair gamester.

And she did hesitate. She sipped her wine, counted her cards, muttered under her breath. She studied her cards, and wrinkled her nose, and frowned at the hidden cards in the stock.

And she played beautifully.

He'd been a fool not to have seen it before. He'd wanted to protect her from card sharps? By heaven, she *was* one. And with her youth and pretty face, and her father's history, she was just the sort of player no one would suspect.

She'd certainly taken him in.

He saw her lead down her diamonds —ace, king, knave, eight. Then she moved on to clubs.

He waited.

Sure enough, just when Malkham played his final card, one he was certain was a winner, she brought out the queen of diamonds.

He had to admire her technique. She'd set them both up the previous week, just the way a sharpster lured in his prey. She'd sent clear signals about how she played, and now she was taking advantage of their erroneous conclusions.

She had challenged his wits, and won over two hundred guineas from him. But did she realize that Malkham was not likely to take losing with such a good spirit? Did she know who she was playing with?

He could see Malkham's minute hesitation as Atalanta scooped up the final trick with her queen. If he figured out her game, she was lost. She didn't play at the level of a man like Malkham.

Or did she? Was she winning merely because of her trickery, or was her skill that much greater than she pretended?

He kept his attention on the game. She didn't do anything strange for another minute or so, and then he heard a small "Oh" from her.

She licked her upper lip nervously, then glanced at Malkham, as if hoping he hadn't noticed.

He had, of course, but he was staring down at his hand as if his opponent were the last thing on his mind.

Then quickly and quietly, she moved a card from the right side of her hand to the left.

Stoke stared at her. He'd fallen for that. She hadn't even been that subtle with him, either. Had she spotted him for a fool? Or had she been playing games with him, seeing how far she could go before he noticed?

If that had been her game, she'd clearly won. She'd misdeclared her hand, losing herself a measly two points, and because of that capotted him for an extra forty points and the game.

He waited to see if Malkham would fall into her trap. He could see the man's eyes flicker just the least bit.

Then he took the bait. But it seemed the lovely gamester was playing it straight this hand. Lulling his suspicions, perhaps?

After the third hand, Miss James was ahead by about ten points, and it all seemed to be luck. She was that good.

The fourth deal was Malkham's, and Atalanta discarded five cards.

She squinted at her hand, and seemed to be counting mentally. Finally, she said "Point of six."

"Good."

Six points to her, then. She stared at her cards again. "Sequence of six. I mean, quint."

There was a slight stir around her, and she looked up as if puzzled. "Isn't that right?" she said.

No one said anything, so Stoke took pity on her. "A quint is a sequence of five, Miss James."

Then he realized what he'd done. She knew what she was doing, and she didn't need anyone's pity, least of all his. She had his two hundred guineas, and might turn it into four hundred before the night was out.

She could actually support herself on winnings like that, until the news of her skill—or her luck—got out. Either way, she couldn't run this rig for long.

But how long did she want?

Her eyes met his, and he thought he detected a spark of amusement there. So she knew he was on to her? Did she find it entertaining?

"I beg your pardon, Lord Malkham," she said. "I meant to say a sequence of six. Just pretend I said it in Latin."

It wasn't Latin, of course, which she must know full well.

"Good," came Malkham's terse reply.

She only needed eight more points in her hand to repique him. If she got that, she'd win the game, and a good chunk of money.

If she didn't have a repique, of course, she could still hope for a pique.

He found the sweat breaking out beneath his tight cravat. Blast the thing, anyway. Who invented such a ridiculous article of clothing as a piece of starched fabric next to the neck?

But he knew his nervousness was due to the cards, not his clothing.

She scowled at her cards. "Three aces?" she said.

She wasn't likely to repique him without four of a kind.

Malkham gave no sign of being relieved. The man must know what her cards were, then.

Or think he did. "Good," he said, as if unconcerned that she might best him in the match.

"Then that's three points for my aces," she said. "And I have four tens, so that's, uh . . ."

She glanced vaguely about at the gawking bystanders, her expression one of abstraction. The crowd stirred, laughter and excitement running through them as they realized she had just repiqued Lord Malkham.

By God, she was good.

"Is that four or fourteen?" she asked, as if she didn't even know that four tens beat three aces.

Malkham's voice was a low rasp. "Fourteen."

She gave Malkham a blinding smile. "Oh, then that means I—"

If she said "pique," she might lose Malkham. Even he couldn't believe she was so ignorant.

She wrinkled her forehead. "I repique you, don't I?" At the assenting murmur from the crowd, her eyes lit up. "I got a repique! I didn't think—" She paused, as if realizing she sounded fatuous. She dropped her eyes to her cards. "I repiqued Lord Malkham," she said with quiet delight, as if she were a schoolgirl staying up late to play cards with the adults.

"Shall we play?" asked Malkham.

She blinked at him for a second, then led out an ace.

Her play was predictable and unexciting. She took the majority of the tricks, and ten bonus points, but she pulled nothing particularly cunning in the play of the cards.

And that was the game, of course. "My win," she said, a pleased grin on her face. "And that's . . . how much? Sixty plus ten, plus six, plus . . ."

"You win seventy-three guineas," said Malkham serenely.

She glowed. "It's like winning a fortune," she said. "I could get to like this."

She cocked her head to one side, looking at Malkham with sparkling eyes. "Do you want to play another game?"

He looked unconcerned, but Stoke knew he must want to win the money back. "If you wish. Shall we double the stakes?"

"Yes, let's."

Stoke felt like he was watching a battle between gladiators. The combatants were strong, and the contest was absorbing. But one of them was fated to be slaughtered, and he didn't want to see it happen.

He didn't know Miss James at all, it seemed, but he still felt something for her. He had no idea why, but he did. She might be a liar, a dissembler, and a cardsharp, but her spirit and passion gripped him.

But how could he tell where the false Atalanta ended, and the real Atalanta began?

In any case, he didn't want to see her lose. She had little enough money to start with, and despite her sophisticated methods, he was sure the loss would devastate her.

On the other hand, if she made an enemy of Lord Malkham, there was no telling what he might do. He was a cunning, dangerous man, and Stoke didn't want to see her hurt by the vulture.

But he couldn't look away. Whatever the outcome, he had to see it.

Though he couldn't have said why.

Chapter Ten

*A*talanta couldn't believe her luck. She'd known she would be able to best Malkham eventually, but she hadn't expected the repique to fall in her lap.

She had repiqued Lord Malkham. The words echoed in her head, dancing about.

She had won seventy guineas from him. And that was just the beginning.

Tom's investigating made it seem likely that Malkham would not be happy to lose even seventy guineas. So now her fish was hooked. She could play out her line as long as she wanted, drawing him further and further in, until she had him where she wanted him.

And then he would find out what came of taking on a James. He might have thought he'd ruined her father and disposed of the family forever, but he would soon learn otherwise. Her father's memory and wrongs were not dead as long as she was living, and she would pursue them until she had righted her father's tragic life.

Lord Malkham would see what it meant to underestimate Atalanta James.

The Earl of Stoke sat down in the red velvet chair with a thump.

By God. He'd just watched Atalanta James win five thousand guineas from Lord Malkham and never break a sweat. Was she made of marble? Or just ice?

He certainly wasn't. The armpits of his shirt were wet through to his coat. He'd never been this nervous during his army days, even during the worst battle.

Perhaps the difference was that here he was a spectator, a passive witness, without the ability to do anything to help.

But now that her series of games with Malkham was over, and she had the man's promise of payment in her reticule, she would have to face Stoke. He didn't like her playing him for a fool.

Or whatever she was doing.

He saw her rise from the table and look around dazedly. Her wine glass was still half-full, he noticed. Had she drunk any of it?

He doubted it.

He strode quickly over to intercept her, before she got the bright idea of gaming with anyone else. Five thousand guineas in a night was all he could watch her win without having a heart attack.

"Miss James," he said, reaching out to take her arm.

"Pardon?" She looked down at his hand, as if it had no business touching her.

He removed his hand. "Perhaps you would enjoy some fresh air, Miss James. The drawing room becomes a bit heated this late in the evening."

She studied him, just as she'd studied her cards. He felt like a fool.

Then she tilted her head to the side consideringly. "Very well," she said. "Fresh air might be pleasant just now."

The other drawing room led onto a deep balcony, he knew. He led her through the thickening candle-smoke to the many-paned doors.

It was heaven out here. The air was cool and fresh, and

he felt invigorated just by breathing it into his lungs. A slight breeze wafted over them.

A pale cloud scudded across the sky, revealing a star.

The stars had been his friends in Spain, but they were much harder to see here in England. Near-constant cloud cover was not conducive to sky-gazing.

In the moonlight, Atalanta looked almost otherworldly. Her pale face and light hair made her seem almost the Atalanta of legend, or at least a statue of her.

"Atalanta," he said, tasting the name. "The mythical Atalanta bent to retrieve the golden apples, and by doing so lost the race." He leaned back against the balcony railing. "Do you ever fear you will do that?"

She leaned over the railing, looking down into the garden below. "I'm made of sterner stuff. I have come prepared to ignore all . . . distractions."

"You never find yourself tempted?"

She gave him a cool look. "No."

She was as hard as she was cold, he thought. More like diamond than marble.

He stared up at the sky. "Do you think me a dupe, Miss James?"

She shifted. "Of course not."

Of course not. She could have fooled him. He turned his head to look at her alabaster face. "A flat? A pigeon?"

She wouldn't meet his eyes. "If a man chooses to think me a pathetic card player, why should I feel guilty over it?"

"Why?" She really was outrageous. "Because you pretended to be a pathetic card player. You set me up."

He pushed away from the railing, and began pacing restlessly about the balcony. "Do you know what that's called, Miss James? Cardsharping is one term. Plucking pigeons. And many other things one cannot mention in the hearing of a lady—even a lady who deserves to be called such things."

He heard the swish of her skirts as she stood up

straighter. "I have done nothing wrong," she said coldly. "And I regret nothing that I have done. Can you say the same for yourself? For your family?"

His family? "You're one to talk. Your father bankrupted you all, and you're on your high horse? Do you think he'd be proud of you, resorting to earning your living by the turn of the card?"

"My father," she said, her voice thick, "is above your scorn. You have no right to talk about him in that way."

"Oh, is that private, then?" He felt his rage building. "Well pardon me for forgetting myself, Miss James. Let me see—when we're in the Park, we share our deepest confidences, but in the evening we turn into strangers again. Is that it? Or did I get too close?"

She looked away. "I have no idea what you're talking about."

"The hell you don't."

He could see the anger building in her face, but he merely crossed his arms across his chest. "Oh, so you think I should moderate my language around you? No swearing before ladies, is that it? Well, I'm not certain I see any about."

She drew back her hand to slap him, and without thinking he grabbed hold of her wrist.

They stood like that for a moment, with him holding her arm. Her chest heaved with her fierce breaths, and her mouth was slightly open, as if she were about to heap reproaches on his head.

Without knowing what he was doing, he jerked her against him and pressed a kiss on her soft mouth.

She froze for a second, as if in surprise. Then she gasped and pulled away, hitting out blindly.

He let go of her at once.

What was wrong with him? He turned away, and strode to the other end of the balcony, hoping to cool his thoughts. Why had he done that? Yes, he was attracted to her—but he wasn't the sort of man to press unwanted advances on ladies. Or any other women, for that matter.

And she was a lady, whatever he'd said. "I apologize," he said, wishing his voice was more steady. "I don't know what came over me."

Her voice was harsh. "It's obvious. You judged me by your personal code of how the world should be, and found me wanting. As if it is your right to judge."

"I—" That wasn't true, was it? "I admit I have a—a sort of code, as you say. But I do try not to judge others by it, only myself."

"How generous."

He tried to see her face, but she turned away. "But that isn't what this is about, Atalanta, and I think you know it. I . . ." The words weren't easy to say. "I trusted you. I confided in you. I do not do that often. So you can see how—how angry it made me to learn you were playing me for a fool."

"I wasn't—" She brushed back a stray lock that dangled in front of her face. "I did nothing wrong. And—and I never lied to you." She turned to look at him. "You must believe that. I wouldn't do a thing like that."

So what was she playing at? "I thought we were—friends. I don't play that sort of trick on my friends."

"I'm not you!" She spread her hands wide in frustration. "You can't judge me by your standards. How could I ever measure up? You may have endured terrible things in the war, but behind everything you had family, security—things that you knew would survive without you. Things that made sense."

She dropped her hands hopelessly. "You can't know what it was like for us. You can't know the choices one must make in such a case."

That was true. And she was right to say he was judgmental—he'd been told it many a time, and accepted that it was one of his faults.

But somehow that didn't make him feel any better. "Don't you feel any guilt? Or do you treat all your friends this way?"

"You don't understand." Her voice was low.

He looked at her, and he knew he would never get rid of her. She would always be in his head, even if he never saw her again. Her eyes, her hair, her sense of humor. Her fire.

What was her hold on him? He didn't know. Perhaps he never would. But he thought he might go mad if he couldn't have her, and to hell with his duty.

"Marry me," he said, before he had the chance to change his mind.

Her eyes widened in surprise. "What?"

There was no going back now. He couldn't withdraw the offer even if he wished.

The realization made him feel free. "Marry me," he repeated. "Your money woes will be over."

That sounded so cold. He cleared his throat, trying to come up with something better to say. "You'll never have to see your cousin Harriet again."

She gave a laugh that sounded half like a sob. "So much for *my* reasons to marry," she said. "But what could you possibly gain?"

You. He thought it so loudly he almost expected her to hear it.

But when he opened his mouth, he couldn't bring himself to say it. "I think we'd go on well together," he said instead. "I can never—never talk to the debutantes I meet. I don't understand their language. But I feel that we—that you and I—can . . . talk."

She turned away again, but not before he saw a tear on her lashes. "I can't marry you." Her voice was ragged.

"Why not?"

What was wrong with her? All her troubles would be over if she were his wife. Surely she couldn't have hoped for even this much to come out of her season.

Of course, she had to take him with the bargain. Perhaps that was the sticking point.

She ran her hand over her hair distractedly, knocking loose her coil of golden braids. "I just can't."

He'd told her his deepest secrets, but she wouldn't tell him anything. He felt his chest tightening, his pulse rising. "I think you owe me more explanation than that."

She shook her head. "You don't want to know."

"Don't tell me what I want." He strode across to her, grasped her shoulder, and turned her around to face him. "I don't have your taste for secrets and surprises, Atalanta. I like things out in the open, where I can see them."

He dropped his hand, but kept his eyes on hers. "That's what I expect of my friends."

"What of your enemies?"

The word hit him like a dousing of ice water. "Enemies?" He couldn't make out her expression in the pale moonlight. "Are you my enemy, Atalanta?"

Her voice was sad. "Yes. I am." She reached up and laid her fingers against his cheek for a moment. "I'm sorry."

Then with a whisper of fabric, she was gone back inside.

Chapter Eleven

*O*nce again, Stoke found himself calling on Atalanta
without really knowing the reason why.

It was ridiculous, really. He'd proposed to her. She'd declared herself his enemy. And now he was coming by for a
chat?

No, not a chat. She was going to tell him why she'd made
such a preposterous accusation, whether she liked it or not.

Once again, Stoke had to wait for the door to be an-
swered. But when the lanky footman finally opened it a
mere six inches, he clearly recognized Stoke. With a nervous start, the lad opened the door the rest of the way and
bowed the earl in.

Stoke had barely stepped into the dingy entrance hall
when he realized he had blundered into the middle of a family crisis.

He saw Atalanta first. She sat on the bottom step of the
worn wooden staircase that led up to the next floor. On her
lap was a child—a girl of seven or eight, perhaps—who
clung to her, weeping.

Stoke recognized Atalanta's cousin Harriet, tight-lipped
and red of face, standing to the side and glaring at the seated
pair. A young man Stoke did not recognize, also rather red,
stood next to Harriet. He had the same angular features and

dun-colored hair as Harriet, but didn't exude the same sharp energy.

No one seemed to notice Stoke. "We have no *room*," Harriet was saying, in the angry tone of someone being ignored. "Where would I put her? And who would look after her? You and Aunt Mathilda are gone half the night at your everlasting card parties, and then you run around all day doing heaven knows what. You can't expect me to look after the child."

Atalanta's face was white and strained as she looked up at her cousin. "I don't." She sounded miserable, almost pleading. "I don't expect anything of you. Louly will be fine here on her own. You know she's quiet."

"I'll not have her skulking about here in her sneaky little way, poking her nose into things behind my back."

The young man put a hand on Harriet's arm in a tentative way. "Now, Harriet—" he began, in a mild voice.

Harriet shook his hand off. "You don't live with her, Lawrence—you don't know what it's like to have her watching you all the time, staring at you with those sharp little eyes. I never know what she's thinking, any more than I do with Atalanta. I'm not putting up with it."

The child looked up from where she clung to Atalanta. Her dark hair was hanging in tangled wisps around her pale, tear-streaked face. "Just for a few days," she said, her voice low. "Please."

Harriet scowled at the girl. "No!"

The child looked up at Atlanta as if she were her last hope. "I can't go back there, Atalanta. I can't. They poured water all over my mattress, and they pull my hair, and Bobby bites me, and then they all laugh."

Harriet snorted. "Carrying tales as usual? And you wonder why the other children don't like you?"

"I tried not telling," said the girl. "I tried, but they just wouldn't stop. Fanny poured ink on my best gown, and when I tried not telling, Cousin Georgiana beat me for it, and they all laughed. And Daphne calls me names. She calls me dwarf, and goblin, and by-blow, and—"

Harriet breathed in sharply. "Daphne would never say such a thing! Oh, for heaven's sake, I can't bear your lies, Louisa. Stop it this instant."

At this the girl began weeping again, large quiet tears that ran down the dirty tracks of her face. Atalanta put her arms around the child, murmuring something into her ear.

The girl clung to her with desperate hands. "I can't," she whispered into Atalanta's neck. "I can't do it anymore, I can't."

Stoke noticed the footman had prudently vanished. He had best make his own presence known before this went any further.

He cleared his throat. "I beg your pardon," he said.

All eyes turned his way.

He couldn't think of anything sensible to say, so he tried to look sympathetic. "Can I help?"

Shocked silence met his words.

Then everyone began talking at once. Stoke could make out few words in the onslaught that followed, but he concluded that Atalanta was surprised to see him there, Harriet was infuriated, and the young man wanted to know who he was.

The last was easy enough. "I am Richard Stanton, Earl of Stoke," he said, stepping toward him and offering his hand. Bowing would be more proper than shaking hands, but it seemed a little late to be playing propriety here.

The young man seemed relieved that someone was talking to him. "Pleasure," he said, taking Stoke's hand in a friendly grasp. "Pleasure. I'm James. Viscount James, that is. Or Lawrence. A lot of people still call me Lawrence."

Stoke hoped this apparently good-natured fellow could help him sort out this scene of chaos. Whether it was Stoke's task to sort it out didn't matter. It was a problem, he was here, and it involved Atalanta—that was all he needed to know.

"Good to meet you," he told the viscount. "So you are brother to Harriet—that is, Mrs. Norris?"

"Yes, that's right," replied the viscount amiably. "And cousin to Atalanta and Louly. I've only just arrived from the country."

So this was the head of the family? A pleasant enough sort, at least at first glance, but perhaps not strong enough to stand up to Harriet's iron hand.

Stoke gave the viscount an understanding look. "I have become something of a friend of, er . . ." Stoke had meant to say friend of the family, but that was an obvious exaggeration. "A friend of Miss James," he said instead. "Perhaps we can discuss whatever the difficulty is, and come to a solution?"

The viscount looked relieved to let him take charge. "Indeed," he said. "Come into the drawing room, we'll have a drink—I'm certain we can figure things out without shouting."

This apparently did not find favor with Harriet. "Lawrence," she said, her voice dripping sarcasm, "you're not going to have a drink? Now?"

The viscount turned and spread his hands in a placating gesture. "Oh, but I need a drink, Harriet. I've been on the road a long time, and I'm tired. Why don't we all have a drink? Do us all some good. Get the child some milk or something. And we can stop shouting, and crying, and all that."

So they all trooped off to the drawing room, the same worn brown room he recognized from before. Tea was ordered up, the viscount poured Stoke a glass of sherry, and everyone found somewhere to sit.

Atalanta, Stoke noticed, sat on a hard chair by the door,

as if preparing to make her escape. She still had Louly—
that was the girl's name, wasn't it?—on her lap, her skirts
wrinkled beneath the girl's weight.

Stoke had no wish to sit next to Cousin Harriet on the
brocade sofa, so he claimed the easy chair by the fire, leaving the viscount to join his stiff-necked sister.

Stoke sipped his sherry and looked at Louly. "Hello," he
said, for a start. He wasn't used to conversing with children,
but surely he could manage. "I'm Stoke. I'm a friend of your
sister's. You're Louly?"

The child nodded.

Not the most promising start. "Is that short for Louisa?"
Another nod. What would get a girl of her age talking? And
what was her age, anyway? "Are you—what—" Best to
guess high, yes? "Nine years old?"

This time she shook her head. Maybe he was frightening
her, but he didn't know what he was doing wrong.

He looked at Atalanta, and she leaned her cheek against
the back of Louly's head. "She's ten, my lord."

Ten? Perhaps she was small for her age. He had the sudden urge to feed her something, as if she were an under-
nourished horse.

He knew he would have a quicker time getting all the
facts from Atalanta or the viscount, but he had a stubborn
curiosity to hear Louly's side of whatever the problem was.
The angry things Harriet had said about her penetrating stare
were partly true—Louly had deep, dark eyes in a peaked
face—but that just gave him an urge to make her smile.

Talking about the weather was out, he supposed. And
politics. He took another sip of his sherry and racked his
brain. "I met your brother the other day."

"You . . . what?" She sounded cautious but hopeful.

"Er, Tom, is that it?" he asked Atalanta, and was met with
a nod. No need to tell the child that Tom had given him the

cold shoulder. "Met him in the Park the other day. Lively fellow."

"You met Tom?" Louly looked up at Atalanta, her face suddenly radiant. "Tom's here? In London? Did you see him? Will I get to see him?"

Atalanta glanced briefly at Harriet, but the older woman just look stony. "Well, Louly," she said, her voice tentative, "if you could stay—"

"That," interrupted Harriet, "is out of the question. For the last time."

It was time he rescued the conversation again. He leaned toward Louly, hoping she felt warmer toward him now that she knew he'd met her brother. "I was wondering, then, Miss Louly. How did you get here?"

Louly's eyes darted toward Harriet as if she were afraid of another scolding, but after a second she said, "I took the stage."

"You—" He paused, taken aback. "You took the stage-coach here, all on your own?"

The child nodded.

He had never heard of such a thing. She would have needed to board the coach at a crowded inn on a major road, only to be deposited at a larger, even more congested inn amid the chaos of London. "And you took a hackney here from Charing Cross?"

"I walked."

"You walked?" He couldn't picture this tiny creature walking for miles in a strange city. "With your luggage?"

The child looked down at her hands. "I didn't bring any."

"Rather spur-of-the-moment then, I see." She might look like a wisp of a thing, but she had her sister's resourcefulness.

He glanced at the pleasant-faced viscount. "And Lord James—you followed her here?"

"That's right," the young man said, starting on his second sherry. "Deduced she would be coming here, so I came in my curricle. Arrived before her, in fact—took her a while to walk from the station, I suppose."

Stoke turned back to Louly. "And then, if I understand rightly, you were hoping to stay here in your cousin Harriet's house for—" Best to be noncommittal. "For a while?"

Louly nodded, but Atalanta raised her chin rather defiantly. "Actually," she said, "it is Lord James's house."

Harriet sniffed. "It is the family townhouse, and it always has been. Not that we get much chance to use it nowadays." She finished with an accusing look at Atalanta.

Atalanta turned her gaze on her young cousin Lawrence. "If you say she can stay, Lord James, then she can," she said with quiet dignity. "You are the head of the family."

Harriet rose angrily from the sofa. "Oh, put on your fine airs, Miss Atalanta James, go ahead. We all know your father was a saint who quoted Latin and Greek when he wasn't buying and selling whole counties. Don't worry about the fact that you can't afford to resole your slippers, no, pay that no mind! *You're* Augustus James's daughter, and don't let anyone forget it! As long as they *do* forget the great Viscount James gambled away all his money—all *my* money, all Lawrence's money, all *everything*—"

The young viscount had risen with his sister, and was ineffectually trying to hush her. She shook him off with an annoyed gesture, but Stoke rose to his feet and held up his hand. "Please," he said. This was getting nowhere. "If I may, Mrs. Norris."

Harriet looked at him through narrowed eyes. "I fail to see what you have to do with any of this."

"Nothing," he said calmly. "But as I happened into the middle of it, and am a disinterested party, perhaps I can help you settle things." He gave her a firm look. "Surely I cannot make things worse than they already are."

"Things are not going to change," Harriet said. She crossed to the drawing room doors, then turned back to face the room again. "That child can stay here for one night. One. That's all. And *you*," she added, turning to Atalanta, "had better keep her out of my way while she's here."

With that, Harriet strode out of the room, closing the white-painted door behind her with a bang.

Stoke was relieved to get Harriet out of the way. "Atalanta," he said, thinking that the viscount was the person he really needed to be dealing with, "I'm sure Louly must be hungry. Why don't you take her to the kitchen and get her something to eat."

Louly's face brightened at that, but Atalanta looked uncertain. "I suppose. . . ." Atalanta said, looking embarrassed. "Lord James—"

"Just call me Lawrence, please," said the viscount, crossing to the sherry decanter once again. "When I hear 'Lord James,' I always think of your father. Besides, it seems a farce to be my-lording a man who can't afford to live in his own house."

He cast a sheepish glance at Stoke. "Treating you like family, you see." Stoke saw the viscount's eyes flicker to Atalanta.

So that's what was going on. The viscount had concluded that he was Atalanta's suitor.

Which, in a way, he was. It seemed strange to recall that he'd actually proposed to her last night. Thank God she'd had the sense to refuse him. He didn't know what he'd been thinking.

In any case, he needed to keep his mind on the current business, which was getting Atalanta and Louly out of the room so that he could talk business with the viscount.

All right, then. Why wouldn't Atalanta want to take the girl to the kitchen?

Of course—the servants. He'd seen their treatment of her before. He cleared his throat. "Lord James—er, Lawrence—perhaps you could escort Miss James and her sister to the kitchen, and personally ask the cook to contrive a good meal for them."

The viscount's rueful nod showed that he caught on right away. "Will do," he said readily, putting down his glass and bowing Atalanta out the door.

Stoke was a bit disconcerted by how quick Lord James was to follow his commands. Either he was so used to being ordered around by his sister that he didn't give it a second thought, or he liked to avoid the burdens that came with decision making.

Stoke only had to wait a minute or two until the viscount returned, looking tired but relieved. "Top off your drink, Stoke? Oh, I see you're still working on it. Do feel free." Lord James looked a bit like a naughty boy. "Don't want to feel like I'm drinking alone, right?"

"Of course." Stoke sipped at his drink to make the young man feel better. "Now then. Is there really no room for the child here?"

"Er, well . . ." The viscount eased himself back down onto the sofa, and sprawled against its back. "She could sleep with Atalanta, of course. Wouldn't be the first time. And she'd cost a sight less to feed than m'horses, let me tell you."

The viscount sighed. "Lord, why do my horses eat so much? It's not like they're out pulling the plow every day. And do you know what horseshoes cost?" He threw Stoke an embarrassed glance. "No, sorry, didn't mean to go on about it. Vulgar to talk about money, I know that—it's just such a fascinating topic when y'don't have any."

He looked a bit sheepish. "So, well, I suppose Louly could stay, in theory. Harriet would never allow it, though. Besides, not sure what my sisters would do without Louly to look after the little ones. My sister Georgiana is having a hard enough time already with Atalanta gone. Even worse is

Harriet being gone—Lord, doesn't seem anyone can control the brats but Harriet. Only person they're afraid of."

That didn't sound good. "So, do you think the other children really are harassing Louly?"

"God, yes. Do it all the time. Harriet keeps them from going too far, but now that she's here—well, all I can say is I'm glad I'm not Louly's age. And you know what else I'm glad of? Glad the brats ain't mine. Hate to think I was responsible for any of the little horrors."

That was plain speaking, to be sure. If the children were half as bad as the viscount claimed, Stoke could see why Atalanta wanted to keep the girl here.

The problem was simple, yet intractable. Harriet was not going to change her mind—that was clear. Atalanta had no power here, and the viscount was obviously unwilling to defy his sister. And yet it would be cruel to send Louly back into such a miserable situation.

Stoke stared into the amber liquid that still half-filled his glass and wondered what to do now.

The thing was, he needed to focus on the battle, not the war. He had no idea how to save Louly from returning to her unhappy home tomorrow, but he knew just how he could make tonight more pleasant for her and Atalanta. For Tom, too, come to think of it.

This would work out perfectly, wouldn't it? Plus give him time to think of a solution.

But . . . wait. Of course. If things went well, he might be on the way to a solution already.

"Are you certain about the elephant, Atalanta?"

Atalanta took a firmer grip on Louly's hair, trying not to hurt the girl too much while brushing out her tangled locks. "That's what Lord Stoke said."

"An elephant! I've never seen an elephant. Do you think one could even fit on the stage?"

Atalanta picked up her scissors and reluctantly snipped out a recalcitrant knot of Louly's dark hair. "London theaters are much larger than anything in Essex," she explained. "Covent Garden Theater seats several thousand people, I believe. And the stage itself has room for hundreds."

Louly let her breath out in a blissful sigh. "Oh, I am so excited! I have never seen anything like it. I'm almost dizzy thinking about it."

Atalanta felt warmed inside to see Louly so happy. "You'll be on your best behavior, of course."

"Of course! I shall say thank you and please, and sir, and I shall sit in ever so ladylike a manner. I won't even chew on my braid."

That made Atalanta laugh. "I should hope not!"

Louly gave a small squeak as her hair caught on the hairbrush.

"Sorry, poppet."

Louly clasped her hands together in front of her. "Atalanta?"

"Yes?"

The question was a few seconds in coming. "Why is Lord Stoke taking us all to the theater?"

Why indeed. Atalanta had been trying to figure that out for the whole five hours since Stoke had issued his unexpected invitation. She and he hadn't exactly parted as friends last night. So why was he trying to help her now?

Did he feel so guilty knowing that his father had helped impoverish her family that he wanted to help her, despite what he thought of her personally? From the hard things he had said last night, she was sure she had lost his good opinion once and for all. She doubted he could ever forgive her for playing him for a fool like that—not that she had thought of it in those terms.

Clearly, he had. Though her lack of honesty, of candor,

might have been worse. That had seemed to bother him more than anything.

"Well, Louly," she said, not sure what to tell the girl, "Lord Stoke is a—a kind man, and he and I have become acquainted while I have been in London. When he learned of your situation, I suppose he wanted to help."

Louly wrinkled up her nose the way she did when thinking hard. "I am immensely grateful that he's taking us to the theater," she said. "But . . ."

Atalanta smiled. "But how is that going to solve the problem?" she suggested.

"Yes! Not that I wish he *wasn't* taking us to see the pantomime. I am very glad for that. But I don't see what it has to do with me wanting to stay here."

Atalanta set down the hairbrush and began braiding Louly's fine brown hair. "It seems Lord Stoke had some extra room in the box at Covent Garden that he had reserved for tonight. When he saw how unhappy you were, I suppose he wanted to give you a treat. In addition . . ." How could she put this politely? "This will also get the two of us out of the house for the evening, so that we—er—do not disturb Cousin Harriet."

Louly held her hands tightly before her. "But then I go back?" she asked in a small voice.

Atalanta wanted to put her arms around Louly and never let her go. "Sweetheart," she said, putting her hands on Louly's shoulders.

"I know, I know." Louly's voice was tight. "She won't let me stay. And there's no one else who'll have me. So I just—go back."

Atalanta leaned forward and put her cheek against Louly's, hugging the girl against her chest. "I still have my plan," she told her sister quietly. "Tom and I have been working on it the whole time I've been here. And I'm getting closer."

Louly's eyes widened. "You are?"

"If I succeed . . ." That "if" always twisted her stomach, she so hated not being certain. "If I succeed, then I can take you away. We'll have our own little house somewhere, and you and I will live there, and Tom, too, when he's home from the army."

"And no Cousin Harriet?"

"And no Cousin Harriet," she said with a rueful laugh. She tried not to speak ill of their relatives to Louly, but sometimes it was impossible.

Louly relaxed against Atalanta and closed her eyes. "No nappies to change, ever again," she said. "No noses to wipe. No more Bobby throwing things, no more Meg pulling hair, no more Daphne saying nasty things about Father and Tom and you—" Louly broke off, and glanced up quickly at Atalanta.

Atalanta smiled. "So she says things about me, too? Don't worry, lambkin. I'm not surprised."

"It doesn't bother you?"

Atalanta kissed her sister on the side of her head. "Louly, Father was a noble man. He was learned, and gentle, and kind. He was always scrupulously honest, but managed to rarely speak ill of anybody. The neighbors, the tenants, the servants—everyone respected him. When they bowed to him, they meant it. He did have his weaknesses, but I have always been proud to be his daughter. So if Daphne Norris insults him and me in the same breath, I'm honored to be in such company."

There was a brisk rap on the door and the upstairs maid, Maggie, looked in. "Parcel downstairs," she said, leaving the door ajar when she left.

Atalanta realized she was expected to carry her own packages up. "I wonder what—" she began, when her cousin Lawrence appeared in the doorway, a large box in his hands.

"Well, now," he said, a big smile on his face. "Look what just came for Miss Louisa James."

Louly stared. "For me?"

Atalanta smiled at the viscount. "Thank you for carrying it up, Lawrence."

He gave an awkward chuckle. "Can't have Lord Stoke think we neglect you, now can we?"

He set the box down on the bed, and Louly ran over to stare at it. "It does say my name." She sounded breathless. "May I open it, my lord?"

"Of course, of course." The viscount helped Louly undo the string that held the box shut, then opened the flaps that protected the contents.

Reverently, Louly lifted a dark blue dress out of the tissue paper that surrounded it. "Oh, Atalanta!" she cried.

It was indeed lovely. There was nothing fancy about it, but it was made of fine wool with beautiful workmanship. A generous amount of deep blue fabric hung straight down from the shoulder in careful pleats, finished off with white ribbon at the sleeves and neck.

Atalanta peered into the box. "Look, Louly, there's more!"

They unearthed a matching coat and hat to go with the dress, and Louly's eyes grew huge in her pale face. "This is so beautiful," she breathed. "I have never owned anything like this! I had not wanted to say it, but I was afraid people were going to laugh to see me in my old clothes at the theater."

Atalanta was amazed that such a thing would even occur to a man like Stoke. "Look, there's a note," she said.

Louly took up the small enclosure and read it quickly. "Lord Stoke says this is a small gift—small!—with his aunt's compliments, and Mrs. Knowles—his aunt, do you think?—looks forward to hosting our party at the theater this evening."

The viscount gave Atalanta a meaningful look. "Now,

that's quite a nice little gift, Louisa. Be sure to thank your sister's beau when you see him."

Atalanta felt her face heat. "He isn't my beau, Lawrence. He's just—we have merely—" There was no way to explain it. "Our fathers knew each other. I believe Lord Stoke feels—feels an obligation due to the fact. That's all."

"Of course, of course," said her cousin, his tone jocular. "Mum's the word." He gave her a wink.

She didn't like the sound of that. "You don't think that Lord Stoke and I—that he would—"

"I don't think anything at all, you can rely on that. Not one to judge, no indeed."

Heavens, he thought that Stoke was aiming to set her up as his mistress. "For mercy's sake, Lawrence, do you actually think I would even entertain the notion of— When has my behavior ever led you to believe that I—"

Lawrence held up his hands in protest. "The fellow has to want something, cousin. And seems to me he can do better than a penniless chit with a reputation for card playing if it's a wife he's looking for."

Louly looked up. "A wife? Atalanta, is Lord Stoke courting you?"

"No!" If only they would all just leave this ridiculous subject alone. "No, Louly, and no, Lawrence—Lord Stoke is nothing more than a friend of the family, and I'm certain he means nothing romantic in my direction."

She flushed at the memory of his sudden kiss last night, but thrust the thought away. Such a thing was impossible for both of them, now or ever. And if he didn't know it by now, she certainly did.

She meant to enjoy tonight to the utmost, and to make sure Louly had a splendid time. But when tomorrow came, she and Stoke would be enemies again. She owed it to her father, to Tom, to Louly.

And to herself.

Chapter Twelve

*A*talanta James was a mystery. Stoke knew that with certainty as he sat across from her in the open carriage.

He saw how her little sister leaned against her, as if drawing on her strength. Atalanta certainly had enough to spare. But what was her aim?

And did he really want to know?

"Are you comfortable?" he asked, before realizing that he had asked them the same thing just a minute before.

Atalanta seemed not to notice. "Yes, thank you, Lord Stoke."

Louly, her dark eyes big in her pale face, nodded her agreement enthusiastically.

As the barouche turned the corner into Bow Street, Stoke pointed out the left side. "Take a look," he told Louly.

Louly and Atalanta crowded together to get their first glimpse of the new home of the Theatre Royal, Covent Garden. Four giant white columns supported a portico over the entrance, flanked on both sides by the theater's representation of the history of drama.

He indicated the figures that adorned the left side of the facade. "These two gentlemen are Shakespeare and Milton," he said. "The odd-looking crew following Shakespeare about are some of his characters. That's Lady Macbeth there, and the hunched creature on the end is Caliban. But alas, no Hamlet."

Atalanta gazed at the variety of figures. "I daresay Hamlet was too high-minded to join this company of villains. Or perhaps he just wouldn't sit still long enough for his likeness to be taken."

Their coachman brought the team to a halt in front of the portico, and the red-and-white liveried footman jumped down to open the door. Stoke descended first. He clasped Louly's slender figure and lifted her down, noting how light the child was. He then offered his hand to Atalanta and helped her down from the barouche.

From the portico above them came a shout. Stoke put his hand to his side reflexively, but of course no sword hung there.

Nor was there any need for one. "Louly!" called the blue-coated lad who bounded down the wide flight of steps toward them. Stoke recognized Atalanta's brother, Tom, as he leapt down the last few steps and embraced Louly in a great bear hug. "How's my Louly-Lou? How is my plum duff?" The lad lifted Louly off her feet and whirled her around. "Oh crikey, you're heavy! You must be big as a hundred-gun man o' war with all its provisions on board." Tom pretended to stagger under Louly's weight. "I know! You must be the elephant I've come to see."

The moment Louly had laid eyes on her brother, her face had lit up with sheer joy. Now she couldn't stop giggling, her arms tight around Tom's neck.

Atalanta watched Tom and Louly with such love in her eyes, and with such an open, unguarded smile on her face, that Stoke couldn't tear his gaze away. How could this artless creature before him be the same young woman who had duped him last night?

After making a great show of being brought to his knees, Tom released Louly with an exaggerated sigh of relief. He bounced back to his feet, and turned to look at Atalanta. "You must be so proud of your little elephant, Miss James."

Atalanta leaned over to brush the dirt off of the knees of Tom's trousers. "Yes, indeed. It's my big elephant who causes all the trouble."

Tom grinned at Stoke. "I wish I *were* a big elephant. I know a few masters I'd like to step on."

As if just now realizing who he was talking to, Tom's grin faded into an embarrassed expression. The lad glanced at the ground, took a deep breath, and raised his eyes again to meet Stoke's. "Tom James," he said after a moment's pause, holding out his hand.

Stoke grasped the boy's hand. "Good to meet you."

Tom gave an awkward sort of shrug. "And—well, thank you for inviting me along tonight. Couldn't have seen Louly much if you hadn't. Appreciate that."

"Glad to have you along. My younger brother, Edmund, will be joining us eventually, so it seemed sensible to invite Atalanta's—er, Miss James's—brother, too."

Under Tom's direct gaze, Stoke felt a bit like an awkward schoolboy himself. He just wished he didn't have to keep explaining his strange relationship with Atalanta.

In any case, he didn't owe an explanation to a boy who was hardly old enough to be shaving yet.

Nevertheless, he found himself hoping that Tom didn't ask.

He gestured up the steps toward the grand doors above them. "Ladies, gentleman, our box awaits."

When Atalanta stepped into the box, she almost gasped at the sight before her. Three tiers of sparkling glass chandeliers fronted the three levels of boxes, their candle-flames gleaming off the golden wreaths which ornamented the box-fronts, and the slender golden pillars that supported each grand circle. The heavy curtain that hid the stage was crimson, and the seats in each box were royal blue, lending the brilliant scene a dramatic air.

"Oh," she breathed. "Oh, Louly, isn't this beautiful?"

Louly moved to the front railing and peered over, then turned back to Atalanta, her eyes huge. "I've never seen such a—a magnificent place. This is like a palace—like Cinderella's palace or something."

Stoke moved to Louly's side. "Mr. Kemble spent so much money building this new theater after the old one burned down, that he had to raise the prices. And do you know what?"

Louly gazed up at him, her attention caught. "What?"

"There were riots over the new prices. Weeks and weeks of riots. Hard to imagine riots in this place, isn't it?"

He caught Atalanta's eye and grinned. A sudden wave of longing washed over her, catching her by surprise.

No, this wouldn't do. This would *not* do. She had to keep her feelings for Stoke under control—she had no other choice.

Stoke's gaze dropped back to Louly, and Atalanta felt stupidly weak. Well, she would just have to get over it, that's all there was to it. She owed it to Tom, and to Louly.

And to her father.

She moved closer to Tom, who stood hesitating at the back of the box. "Thank you," she said in a low voice, putting her hand on his arm. "I want tonight to be perfect for Louly, so thank you for coming along, and being civil to Lord Stoke."

Tom fidgeted a bit. "Still don't understand what you're playing at," he said. "Seems to me you're friends or you're foes. Can't be both. Not to my mind, anyway."

Atalanta gave a small sigh. "I am friends with the man, but an enemy to—to his father. And his family, too, in a way."

Tom wrinkled his brow. "I suppose I can see it. Brutus

and Caesar were bosom friends, after all, but Brutus still had to snuff out the old fellow."

Atalanta couldn't suppress her grin. "And they say you aren't a scholar?"

The curtains at the back of the box parted, and a round little woman entered followed by an elegant young man.

Stoke crossed to the new arrivals. "Good evening, Aunt," he said, kissing the plump woman on the cheek. "May I introduce Miss James, Mr. Thomas James, and the charming Miss Louisa James?"

He turned to Atalanta. "This is my aunt Mrs. Knowles, reputed to be the most amiable lady in Hampshire. And this," he indicated the gentleman, "Is my brother, Mr. Edmund Stanton."

As she made her curtseys, Atalanta decided that Edmund Stanton was likely the typical young buck-about-town he had seemed at Lady Isabella's—fashionable, stiff, and slightly bored.

Mrs. Knowles, on the other hand, looked rosy and comfortably ordinary—the image of a country grandmother, full of hugs and hot porridge.

Stoke's aunt greeted them warmly, though she gave Atalanta a searching glance. Edmund bowed correctly, and cast a rather patronizing smile on Tom's answering bow.

Stoke ushered his aunt to a seat in the front of the box. He insisted that Atalanta and Louly join her in the front, and he and the other two men sat in the row behind them.

Atalanta found herself in between garrulous Mrs. Knowles and Louly, who sat shyly on her other side. Just a few minutes of the older lady's friendly conversation had Atalanta chatting away about everything from plays she had seen as a child, to the best way to get mustard stains out of silk.

Atalanta wished she had some way to get Louly talking, but she knew better than to press the girl in such a situation.

Tom was silent too, sitting behind Louly, occasionally tugging on her braids to make her giggle.

Luckily, before Atalanta could worry overmuch about her siblings, the curtain was rung up for the first piece.

If Atalanta could have chosen what plays were performed that evening, she could have arrived at none more certain to please Louly than those they saw. The first play was a Gothic melodrama by Monk Lewis called *Adelmorn the Outlaw.* This tale full of ghosts, duels, and dungeons held her sister spellbound.

Atalanta occasionally heard a snicker from Tom at some of the more ridiculous plot developments, but she could tell that most of the other audience members were enjoying the play as much as Louly. When the hero and his ladylove pledged their eternal devotion in an extended and rather overwrought scene, Tom snickered again, and poked Atalanta.

"What?" she whispered.

Tom leaned close to her. "If our hero isn't a murderer, isn't it a bit odd that he doesn't remember it? Dashed convenient for the playwright, don't you know?"

Atalanta hid her smile. "Hush now," she whispered, indicating Louly's quiet absorption.

But Tom just poked her again. *"What?"*

"Do Bavarian castles really have secret passages everywhere? If so, why do they always lead to the dungeons? If I were building a secret passage, it would lead to the kitchens. Grab a midnight snack, no one the wiser."

Atalanta was trying to come up with some way to quiet her brother when Stoke tapped him on the shoulder. "Mr. James."

Tom looked a bit apprehensive. "Sir?"

Stoke handed Tom several silver coins. "Buy your sisters something to eat, scamp. And yourself as well, if you behave."

"Yes, sir!" Atalanta was embarrassed to note that Tom counted the money before slipping it into his waistcoat pocket. He bounced up from his seat, turned to go, and then stopped. "Which way is the coffee room?"

In the end, Stoke drafted Edmund to show Tom the way. Atalanta breathed a sigh of relief when the two young men left, and the box grew quiet again.

Tom and Edmund were not back in five minutes, nor ten. After twenty minutes, Atalanta stopped looking for them every time footsteps sounded in the passageway behind the box.

The play was well into the fourth act when the young gentlemen finally reappeared. Tom was in the lead, carrying a tray laden with glasses and decanters. Edmund followed with a basket of fruit and a tray full of jellies.

Tom set his tray down on the small table at the side of their box. "Beware Greeks bearing gifts," he said, sounding smug.

"Oh, Tom!" cried Louly, her eyes shining. She cast a shy glance at Lord Stoke. "Thank you very much."

Stoke smiled at the girl. "You are most welcome, Miss Louly." He turned his gaze to Tom and Edmund. "Was there a queue stretching out the door and all the way to Hampstead Heath?"

Tom and Edmund exchanged a guilty glance. Tom cleared his throat. "We . . . got lost." The mischievous grin on his face belied his words.

Edmund frowned at Tom. "Actually, had a few friends to say hello to. Didn't think you lot would starve in the meantime."

Atalanta gave Tom a skeptical look. She could tell he was hiding something, but whether from her or from Stoke, she couldn't tell. She resolved to get the truth out of him, or at least try.

Mrs. Knowles bustled over to the refreshments and proceeded to pour the drinks. Atalanta took advantage of the moment to pull Tom aside. "What's going on?"

Tom glanced around the box as if seeing whether anyone was in earshot. Apparently satisfied, he leaned closer to her and lowered his voice. "Malkham's here."

Atalanta felt her heart sink. It was a perfect opportunity, but she found herself wishing she could have had just this one night for herself. One night without any worries, any schemes, any thoughts of the task before her.

But those were selfish thoughts. She had spent years preparing to take on Lord Malkham and his confederates, and she refused to lose her nerve now that she was so close to her goal.

She gave Tom a slight nod, then turned to Stoke. "It is a little warm in here, my lord," she said, trying to sound casual. "Tom has offered to walk with me as I get a bit of fresh air."

Stoke gave them a doubtful glance. "I would be happy to accompany you, Miss James."

Atalanta gave an airy wave of her hand. "Tom is not interested in the play, and doesn't much care to be cooped up. We shall do fine, my lord."

She only wished she felt as confident as she sounded.

Stoke stared down at the stage without seeing a thing. Miss Atalanta James had done it again. Whatever intrigue she planned, whatever piece of duplicity she intended, she clearly felt no compunction at using his hospitality to further her designs.

He needed more information.

Pretending he was going to refill his wineglass, he joined Edmund at the back of the box. "So," he said, his voice mild, "what was it you and Tom did while you were gone so long?"

Edmund turned and gave him a disbelieving look. "Are you checking up on my movements?"

Why was talking with Edmund always so difficult? "It's not *your* movements I'm worried about."

"Oh." Edmund digested that for a moment. "Don't precisely see why you care, but suppose that's not my lookout." He gave a slight shrug. "Took young James backstage, introduced him to a few actresses I know."

One hour's acquaintance and Edmund was already corrupting Atalanta's little brother. "What am I supposed to tell Miss James? That my invitation to the theater included a tour of the actresses' dressing rooms?"

Edmund rolled his eyes. "Deuce take it, it's not like they were naked."

So, where were Atalanta and Tom now? He doubted that Tom was introducing his sister around in the green room.

"Did you go anywhere else?"

"What, do you think I had time to take him on a trip to the local brothels and gaming hells?"

Stoke closed his eyes for a moment, gathering his patience. "Just tell me where you went, and everything you did."

"Nothing," Edmund said, the annoyance evident in his voice. "We walked through the box lobby, and the saloon, and the green room. That's it. Said hello to a few friends. We didn't drink, we didn't wager, I didn't introduce the kid to opium or to moneylenders, and I didn't sell him into slavery."

"All right, all right. You're saints, the two of you."

"Are you done, then?" Sarcasm dripped from every syllable. "May I watch the remainder of the play, your lordship?"

Maybe in a few years they would be able to talk to each other like human beings. But clearly not yet. "Go ahead," he told his brother, knowing he would get no more information from that quarter.

Edmund sauntered over to a chair on the right side of the box and settled languidly into it.

The play, it seemed, had reached a dramatic moment. Surprisingly realistic-looking lightning flashed across the stage as the deep sound of thunder boomed through the theater. Louly jumped in her seat. He realized that at some point his aunt must have moved to the chair next to Louly, because now she put her arm around the girl's shoulders. Louly didn't respond at first, but after a few seconds she seemed to melt against the motherly figure.

Stoke felt a sudden rush of anger at Atalanta's relatives. What was wrong with them? The child acted like she hadn't been hugged in months. Was it so hard to show her a little affection, even if she was the daughter of the man they blamed for their misfortunes?

He could see why Atalanta wanted money. She must be aching to take her little sister out of the miserable situation she was in and give her a real home. But surely there was a better way than turning cardsharp.

Stoke leaned against the wooden wall of the box and pondered. He had to admit he preferred black and white, good and bad, right and wrong. He hated dealing with gray.

And for all her golden hair and blue gowns, Atalanta James was as gray as could be. No, not gray. Black and white tangled together, perhaps inseparably.

He shook his head and moved to take a seat in the second row of the box. This sort of thinking would get him nowhere. Dash it, he would rather be doing something—anything—than hanging about in this limbo of indecision.

For that's what it was—indecision. The sort that got men killed on the battlefield. He couldn't decide if Atalanta was honorable. He couldn't figure out what she was up to.

And he sure as hell couldn't nail down how he felt about her.

So where was she now, she and that brother of hers? He idly ran his eyes over the other boxes. The theater was filling up now that the half-price patrons had been admitted, and the pit and galleries were filled to bursting. The boxes were more sedate, though the ladies' colorful satins and silks were lively next to the men's more restrained clothing.

As his gaze passed over the side boxes, one particular shade of blue caught his eye. He looked back, and there she was.

For a second he wondered if he could be mistaken, but no such luck. There she stood, Miss Atalanta James, in Lord Malkham's box, conversing nonchalantly.

He could make out Tom behind her, but he couldn't quite tell if . . . no, there he was. They were clearly talking to Malkham himself.

That was it. He would get the truth out of her this time, no evasions, no half-lies. He might be a patient man, but even he had his limit.

And Miss Atalanta James had just pushed him to it.

After leaving Lord Stoke's box, Atalanta and Tom searched through the saloon where Tom had spotted Malkham, to no avail. They didn't know which box was his, but Tom knew how to find out—he'd discovered a perfect spot at the front of the theater from which one could see every box.

A quick trip to Tom's spot gave them the information they needed, and before long they were hesitating outside the red curtain that separated Malkham's box from the lobby.

Atalanta hated not knowing what to do. "I don't suppose one knocks," she said hesitantly to Tom.

"No place *to* knock—or scratch, for that matter. Just walk in, I suppose."

Gathering her courage about her, Atalanta pushed aside the crimson curtain and stepped into the box.

Lord Malkham was not alone. A handful of young gentlemen who looked fresh from the country lolled about, interspersed with colorful ladies— No, she realized after a second, these were certainly not ladies. Women, then— rouged, laced, perfumed women with smiling lips and cold eyes.

"Lord Malkham," she said, trying not to sound like a schoolgirl, "may I have a word with you?"

Malkham's dry, wrinkled face looked up, and he gave her a withered smile. "Miss James," he said. "What a—*pleasant* surprise." He looked at Tom. "Oh, have you brought your puppy dog with you?"

Atalanta tried to swallow the tightness in her throat. "I believe, sir, you owe me some money."

His eyes narrowed. "And you think to dun me at the theater? How quaint." The women in the box tittered. They obviously found this exchange more interesting than the play, and Atalanta felt awkward having everyone stare at her so.

"The question is not whether I am quaint, or countrified, or anything else," she told him calmly, "but whether you pay your debts of honor promptly." She favored the other men in the box with a quick glance, then turned her gaze back to Malkham. "I trust you do not wager with money you do not have? I should not think you would care to earn such a reputation."

She could see she had hit a nerve. Good. Now to reel him in.

"Of course I pay my debts, girl." Malkham's voice was curt, but she could detect an undercurrent of tension. "Anyone could tell you that."

"Very good. I trust the draft on your bank will be in my hands by tomorrow morning?"

She could see a muscle twitch next to his eyelid. "If that's really what you want."

She felt a wave a relief pass through her. She had him. She could feel Tom relax behind her.

Of course, she couldn't let Malkham see he was playing into her hand. "What do you mean?" she asked, trying to sound the slightest bit uncertain.

His smile widened, showing his yellow teeth. "I challenge you to a rematch. At Lady Isabella's, next week. Double—or nothing."

She paused a second before replying. "No, I don't think so," she said, trying to sound tempted. "I think it's best if I stop now."

He shook his head as if disappointed in her. "Your father would not have stopped."

It actually hurt to keep her polite smile. To hear him talking about her father like that, after everything Malkham had done—she found it hard to bear. "I suppose . . ."

"Yes?"

"Do you play whist, my lord?"

Malkham smiled until she could see his pale gums. "I play everything, my dear."

Atalanta gave him a small nod. "I know my father lost a sum of money to you and to a Sir Geoffrey Yarrow at whist. I admit I have a whim to try to win some of it back. If you can prevail upon this Sir Geoffrey to partner you at whist, I will gladly play you again."

Malkham's eyes narrowed. "An odd request."

"Perhaps it is. Perhaps I am odd, too. But I follow my whims whenever I can."

Atalanta turned away and stepped toward the back of the box. Tom followed her soundlessly. When she reached the crimson curtain, she glanced over her shoulder at Malkham.

She gave him a bland smile. "I am afraid that for you, Lord Malkham, it's pay or play. Whist next week with Sir Geoffrey, or five thousand guineas tomorrow morning. Your choice."

With that she pushed aside the curtain and stepped through it.

She hardly dared to breathe until she was several boxes away from Malkham. Then she leaned against a wall, her breath coming in gasps.

Tom grinned at her. "You did it," he whispered, patting her on the shoulder. "That was ripping."

Her heart pounded in her chest. "I can scarcely believe I pulled it off. I was terrified I was going to stammer or something, and give it all away. I could hardly keep my voice from shaking."

"You did fine." Tom glanced down the corridor. "Looks like the first play's finished. We'd best be getting back."

The worst was over. Now perhaps she could enjoy the rest of the evening. It was the last time she would spend with Louly for a long while, and she wanted to make the most of it.

It would also be one of the last times she and Stoke would meet as friends. She felt time slipping away from her, and was helpless to stop it.

Chapter Thirteen

*B*y the time Atalanta and her brother finally returned, Stoke was the only occupant of the box. He watched Atalanta part the curtain and step through almost hesitantly, Tom following close behind. When her eyes took in the empty chairs, Stoke thought she looked a bit embarrassed.

"Welcome back, Miss James," he said. He nodded to her and to Tom.

She gave him a hesitant smile that made him want to forgive her everything. "Has Louly—is Louly out with Mrs. Knowles?"

He saw Tom heading for the food, and recalled when he'd been sixteen and always hungry. "My aunt has taken Louly to the ladies' retiring room. They should be back momentarily."

"Oh, thank you. That was kind of her."

She gave him another smile, and he realized her whole face changed when she did that. In repose, she could look severe, sad, even cold, but when she smiled, she suddenly looked very young and vulnerable.

He had meant to accuse her as soon as she returned to the box, to tell her he'd seen her with Malkham, but somehow he didn't have the heart to do it. "Would you like some more wine, Miss James? Or some fruit?"

"Is there any lemonade left?" she said, moving toward the refreshments as if she expected to serve herself.

"Certainly." He poured a glassful and handed it to her as she reached the table.

"Thank you." She glanced around the box. "I don't know if I ever thanked you properly, Lord Stoke, but this is—" She waved her hand, indicating the entire theater. "This is all so splendid. Such a wonderful evening."

He tried not to think of the fact that she'd spent part of her wonderful evening with Malkham. "You are most welcome, Miss James. My aunt has enjoyed the company, as have we all."

The curtain at the back parted, and Edmund returned from whatever ramble he'd been on. "Ran into Ostenley," he said, picking up his wineglass from where he'd left it on his chair. "Turns out old MacNeath is auctioning some of his prime bloodstock at Tat's. Don't suppose we're in the market?"

With all the confusion over whether he owed Atalanta a fortune or nothing at all, they were certainly not in the market. "Not this time."

"'Fraid you'd say that." Edmund sipped at his wine, then put the glass right back down. "Dash it, Richard, I hear he's putting Queen of Sheba on the block. Never get a chance like that again."

Tom had been sitting at the front of the box, craning his neck to look at the boxes above them, but this caught his attention. "Queen of Sheba?" he said. "The Queen of Sheba sired by Ptolemy out of Blackbriar?"

"That's right." Edmund looked surprised. "You familiar with the mare?"

"A bit." Tom swung around in his seat so he could face Edmund. "Ptolemy was one of ours. Fast as the blazes. What do they think Queen of Sheba will go for?"

So that was the way to win over Atalanta's brother. The entire family was clearly horse-mad.

Of course, Stoke thought, he should have deduced that. Atalanta had told him about Tom losing his beloved horse, Icarus. Icarus, whom he had called Henry's Folly, and on whose strong back he had ridden in more than one battle.

Had Atalanta told Tom that? Was that why he acted resentful much of the time?

He watched Tom as the conversation with Edmund continued, but he couldn't tell. He glanced over at Atalanta, but she was watching Tom, a sad smile on her face.

As if feeling his eyes on her, she looked up and met his gaze. Her face seemed to brighten for a moment, then she looked away.

In the end, Edmund invited Tom to accompany him to Tattersall's the next day to see the horse auction. Stoke was glad enough the two young men had found a mutual interest—a *harmless* mutual interest—but he was not going to buy the horse for all that.

He heard a high, animated voice out in the corridor. The crimson curtain parted, and his aunt and Louly came in, holding hands.

Atalanta rose to her feet. "I'm sorry I put you to such trouble, ma'am—" she began, but the plump woman interrupted her.

"Heavens, dear, don't think of it. And do call me Aunt Knowles—I would so much enjoy it—I was just telling Louly how I like to pretend I am an aunt to all the world, and I cruelly insist everyone I like addresses me as such."

Louly glowed. "Atalanta," she said in her soft voice, "Aunt Knowles was just telling me about a kitten she has. Tiger Lily. She says she can put Tiger Lily in the pocket of her cloak and carry her around, and she never makes a peep. Have you ever heard of a kitten like that?"

Atalanta tugged on Louly's braid. "I once had a kitten

named Louly who chewed the feet off all her dolls. Is that the same?"

Louly giggled as Atalanta sat and pulled her onto her lap. "My kitten, though," Atalanta continued, "got to be so big that she carried me around in her pocket. 'May I come out now?' I would ask, but my giant kitten would just say, 'Not until you've eaten every last little bit of food on your plate!' "

"You're so silly," Louly said tolerantly.

Atalanta had been looking forward to the elephant for Louly's sake, but when it finally arrived she found herself impressed. It was so grand and ridiculous—powerful and almost dignified, but obviously put into the pantomime only to increase the take at the box office.

Louly sat between the two women this time, and Atalanta could see that Stoke's aunt was having as much fun watching the child's excitement as Atalanta was herself.

After the elephant had been onstage for a minute or so, Atalanta felt Stoke lean over the back of her chair. "Don't look now, but young Tom seems as enthralled by the elephant as your sister."

She glanced over at the right side of the box. "I see Edmund is not immune to the elephant's charms either."

Stoke glanced up and then shrugged. "He has always had a liking for actresses."

"And I thought men weren't interested in women who were gray and wrinkled."

All action onstage came to a standstill as the elephant lumbered about. While the children in the audience stared raptly at the beast, Atalanta could hear their elders chatter away.

Stoke pulled his chair close behind hers and lowered himself into it, as if anticipating a lengthy conversation. "Are men all so shallow?"

"I hope not." She realized she didn't actually know that many men. Her life had been very . . . small until now. "Do *you* think men are shallow, by and large?"

He stared off into space reflectively. "Perhaps—perhaps by nature, men tend only to look at a woman's surface. And so later on, they are surprised to find the woman they married is nothing like the woman they—they imagined. But I think men who have some experience of the world learn to look deeper."

She hadn't expected him to answer so seriously, and didn't know quite what to say.

He continued, "I think women learn at an earlier age to look past the facade—perhaps because they have more at risk."

"That seems likely." She turned in her seat to face him, leaning on the wooden chairback. "If I were a man, then I would have attended Eton rather than Tom. After that I could have gone on to Oxford on a King's Scholarship the way I hoped he would, and made useful contacts there, then pursued a lucrative profession. If I were a solicitor, or—or in business of some type—" She had to laugh at her own ignorance. "You can see I know so little of business that I don't even know how to speak of it! But perhaps in banking, or some such career, a person could earn enough to support a family well." She paused for a moment, then added more quietly, "If one were a man."

He reached up to push an errant strand of hair off her face. His fingers were gentle as they touched her cheek, and she felt a strange tingle. "But as you are a woman, you have far fewer ways of raising a large sum of money."

"To remain entirely respectable, I can only inherit it or wed it." She tried to keep the bitterness out of her voice.

"And that is why you game for it?" His tone was grave. "You find you have a talent for the cards, and so you seek a fortune at the tables?"

She turned her eyes back to the stage, unable to meet his honest gaze. "I suppose . . ." She swallowed. "What other choice do I have?"

"There are always choices. Sometimes we just don't see them."

Was he right? Was she mistaken in her belief that winning back her father's money was the only way to right the wrong done to her family?

She looked back at Stoke. His dark eyes showed sympathy and understanding.

But she knew better. Life was not that simple. "If I have so many choices, what are they? You seem to have strong opinions about what I should not be doing, but what would you have me do instead?"

She gripped the back of the chair with tense fingers, and lowered her voice. "What am I to do about Louly, if I have so many choices? It seems I only have one—to send her back where she is horribly unhappy. And Tom—he is determined to do something reckless if I cannot provide him money for a commission by the end of the week. How many choices do I have there?"

Stoke narrowed his eyes. "You won several thousand guineas from Lord Malkham. That is more than enough to buy an army commission, if that is truly what Tom wants." He paused for a moment, frowning. "Does he have his heart set on an army career?"

She felt relieved he had not pressed the issue of the money she'd won from Malkham. "Tom is quite keen on the army," she told him, "and though I know that is common in young men his age, I think it might be just the thing for him. He has so much energy—he can never sit patiently studying, or indeed sit still at all—he must always be off doing this one moment, breaking that the next." She gave a rueful smile as she glanced over at Tom, who stared with great interest at the elephant while at the same time trying to balance his chair on two legs.

When she looked at Stoke again, she saw that his eyes were also on Tom, but he was still frowning. "Is something the matter?" she asked him.

He gave her a considering glance. "So you think the army will channel his energy into a useful path? That giving him responsibility will make a man of him?"

She didn't like the challenge in his voice. "I admit I am no expert on army life, but I have not been able to think of a better choice for him."

Stoke shook his head. "A few years ago I might have agreed with you. That sort of responsibility indeed steadies many undisciplined lads. But how many of them die before the lesson is learned? And how many others die, how many actions fail, because impetuous young officers make poor choices?"

She felt her anger rising. "Then I ask you once again— what choices do I have? What would *you* have Tom do now? Invest in a fraudulent scheme to mine copper in Peru?"

He laughed, and that just made her angrier. "Indeed, that is exactly what he has in mind. A great friend of his has recommended it, and unless I convince him he has better options soon, he will ruin himself that way."

Stoke still looked amused. "And you, with all your intelligence, your cunning schemes, cannot persuade him otherwise?"

She felt frustration boiling within her. "What cunning schemes work on a younger brother? Can *you* keep Edmund on the straight and narrow path? From what I've seen, even with your advantages of title and wealth, you have little ability to influence him, let alone control him. And you expect that I, no actual relation to Tom, alone, without friends or money, and a female, can prevail on him to do what I recommend?"

She was appalled to hear a quaver in her voice. Apparently he heard it too, for he took her hand in a warm grasp. "You are right—it is no laughing matter. Trying to keep someone from ruining his life when he is intent on doing so is an agonizing task."

She could hear the earnestness in his voice, and it disturbed her.

Louly tugged on her arm. "Atalanta, look!"

She turned her eyes back to the stage. The rubber-limbed clown, Grimaldi, was trying to catch the reins of a milky white horse that trotted around him in a circle. "Look at the horse, Atalanta! Isn't it beautiful?"

"Horses and elephants both?" she said, giving the girl a squeeze. "They should call it the Covent Garden Menagerie."

She glanced quickly back over her shoulder, but saw that Stoke had moved to the back of the box.

It was just as well. While she was with Louly, she should give the girl her full attention. Their time together would be all too short.

She did wonder, though, what Stoke had meant by his last remark. Who had he tried to protect?

And against what?

The stars glittered down on them from the midnight sky. From where he sat on the backward-facing bench of the carriage, Stoke watched quietly, not wishing to break the peaceful mood.

The unusually clear sky let through moonlight that illuminated the passengers in the open barouche. Atalanta's golden hair appeared silver in this light, as she looked down at Louly with a sad smile on her lips. The child was fast asleep, slumped against her sister in exhaustion. Atalanta's arm was around the girl, and they were both wrapped in a thick coach rug, though neither seemed to notice the cold. A

breeze blew a few loose wisps of Atalanta's hair about her
face, and Stoke knew he wanted the moment to last.

A night watchman called the hour, and Atalanta looked
up as if recalled to her surroundings. Her eyes met his, and
he thought he saw tears in them.

"Lord Stoke," she said quietly.

His title suddenly sounded needlessly formal to him. He
wished she would call him Richard.

She smiled at him. "I want to say how grateful I am for
tonight."

He hated being thanked. "There is no need—"

"Please—let me. This meant so much to Louly. . . . I
don't know how to express it."

"Believe me, the look on your sister's face when the elephant arrived was all the thanks I need." This was a good
time to change the subject. "By the bye, I have news to tell
you—I didn't want to say it in front of Louly in case you
don't like the idea, but as she's sleeping . . ."

Atalanta looked puzzled. "You have news?"

"You could call it a proposition."

The instant he said the word, he wanted to call it back.
Not that Atalanta would take it to mean he was offering her
a slip on the shoulder—no, worldly as she sometimes
seemed, she was too innocent for that.

It was just that uttering the word "proposition" put such
ideas into his head, and he didn't need to be distracted now.

"My lord?"

Atalanta's voice brought him back to reality. "I beg pardon, Miss James—I must be a bit tired."

She smiled wryly. "I understand completely. So—you
said something about a proposition?"

"An idea, let us call it." He leaned toward her. "You do
not want to send Louly back to your relatives tomorrow. Tomorrow is also when my aunt returns to her country home.
Because her daughter will be away in Ireland for a few

months visiting relatives, my aunt will be sadly alone for that time. She has taken a fancy to Louly, and hopes the child might accompany her when she leaves tomorrow, to stay with her in Hampshire for however long proves convenient for you."

Atalanta looked startled. "I—my lord—"

"Why don't you call me Richard?" That was not what he'd meant to say, and it surprised him. Since when did he speak without thinking?

He did wish she would stop my-lording him. And he had to admit he wanted to hear his name on her lips, not just his title.

She looked flustered. "Well, I—I don't know if—" She pushed a stray tendril of hair off her face. "You say that your aunt—she wants to take Louly with her? To the country?"

Was it so hard for Atalanta to say his name? "She has a nice little place in Hampshire—snug, well-aired, cheerful—and she's very good with children. She had several of her own, and has quite a few grandchildren already, and I know she would enjoy spoiling Louly a bit while Caroline and her family are gone."

"Well, I—this is all so sudden, so . . . unexpected. I don't know what to say."

He smiled at her. "You could try saying, 'Yes, Richard, I would love to.' "

She clenched her hands together in her lap. "I—I am very grateful for the offer. Surprised, and grateful. I never dreamed—it all just seems so . . ."

Why did she look so uncomfortable? "Is there a difficulty? Believe me, Louly will be doing my aunt a favor by keeping her company."

"It's—it's not that." She closed her eyes and took a deep breath, as if she were preparing herself for a difficult task. "I . . . I do not think I can accept."

He felt a surge of anger. "You cannot accept?" This was

ridiculous. "You mean you *will* not. Just as you would not take Keemun. Are you so determined not to owe me anything?"

"You know I could not accept a horse from you. It would be shockingly improper."

"Oh, have you started behaving with propriety? Somehow I missed seeing that. Or perhaps a cardsharp who visits a man of Malkham's ilk in his box at the theater is your idea of a proper lady?"

He expected her to take offense, to say something cutting, but she just pressed her lips together in silence.

"Forget the horse," he said. "I seem to recall I actually proposed to you last night, though I must have been mad at the time. That was another offer from me that you had no trouble refusing. No, you will take nothing from me—neither a horse, nor marriage, nor the happiness of your sister. Any of these would have eased your burdens. But though you are happy to play cards with me—more than happy, in fact—you refuse any attempt to help you. Tell me, are you constitutionally unable to let anyone do anything for you? Or is it just me?"

Atalanta's voice was quiet. "Believe me, you don't want to know."

What was wrong with her? "I swear, you will owe me nothing if your sister goes to stay with my aunt. I don't play games like that."

"I know you don't," she said quickly. "It's just—it's a matter of . . . of honor."

This made no sense. "Honor? Whose honor would be compromised if my aunt took Louly with her?"

She closed her eyes for a moment. "Mine."

"But that's ridiculous." There was something she wasn't telling him. Of course, that was nothing new. "You and I both know that my family owes a debt to you. So how can it be wrong for you to take such a small thing?"

"Because I'm not who you think I am."

That stopped him for a second, but it made no sense. "You're saying you're not Atalanta James?"

"No, nothing like that. But . . ." She looked down at her clenched hands. "But you think that we're . . . friends. You offer to help Louly, and me, with that in mind."

He recalled what she'd said last night. "You claimed you were my enemy. Is that it?"

She gave a small nod.

"My enemy? What have I ever done to you?"

"You are your father's heir."

He couldn't believe he was hearing this. "You call yourself my enemy because my father won money from yours? That's childish."

What sort of bizarre game was she playing? He couldn't read her face. "Is that why you won that money from me?" he demanded. "To get your revenge? Keemun is worth far more than two hundred guineas, let me tell you."

"How much money did your father win from mine? *How* much? And you really thought one horse could buy back your father's sins?"

"Sins?" He wanted to shout at her, break things. "So *you* can win money from me with impunity, but you call my father's winnings a sin?"

"He cheated!" She sat there with her mouth open, staring as if the words had been torn from her chest against her will.

Stoke froze. His chaotic thoughts whirled in his head for a moment, then crystallized into one: How dare she.

Feeling ice running through his veins, he fixed his eyes on hers and wouldn't let her look away. "You don't know what you're saying." His words were cold and deliberate. "You have just made an unpardonable accusation. If you were a man, I would call you out for such slander." He held her gaze unblinkingly. "I suggest you retract it."

She put her hands over her eyes. "I knew you'd take it

this way. That's why I never told you. But it's true, I
swear—I have the proof."

Proof? "What the hell are you talking about?"

She glanced down at Louly. "I can't talk about it here,"
she said in a low voice.

"You'd better talk about it."

She lifted her hands helplessly. "Not here. If you—" She
broke off for a moment. "Could you call around one tomorrow? My cousin should be out. I can explain everything
then."

"What about Louly?"

"What about—" She looked confused. "What do you
mean?"

"What about Louly staying with my aunt?"

She sat there for a second, and he could see the sheen of
tears in her eyes. "You would still—you still want her to
go?" she asked, her voice thick.

"Of course. She has done nothing wrong. What sort of
man would I be if I punished her because I was angry at
you?"

She held a hand to her eyes for a moment, then fumbled
in her reticule and pulled out a handkerchief. She wiped her
eyes, blew her nose, and then stuffed the handkerchief back
into the drawstring bag. "Thank you," she said quietly. "I
don't know how to express my gratitude."

Really. "You could start by taking back your accusation."

"I—I can't. You know I can't. You keep telling me you
value honesty. Do you really want me to lie to you?"

She really must believe what she was saying. "You said
you have something in your possession which you think
constitutes proof?"

"Yes. If you can call on me tomorrow, at about one, I can
show it to you, and explain everything."

He ought to refuse her request, of course. He shouldn't
dignify her slander with an audience.

But somehow he couldn't turn his back on her. Not yet. "Very well," he said. "But I shall expect a full explanation at that time. And keep in mind the seriousness of your charge, Miss James."

"Don't worry." Her eyes looked haunted. "I know full well what I'm saying."

Chapter Fourteen

Atalanta's stomach churned when she heard the tap of the door-knocker. She was perfectly in the right—in fact, she was the injured party. So why was she so dreading the coming interview?

Because she was going to hurt Stoke, that was why. Stoke, the man who had somehow convinced his aunt to carry Louly off to the country this morning, to sleep in a soft warm bed and be doted on by the motherly woman.

She heard the front door open with a squeak and a groan. Then muffled voices came from the front hall, and she felt a waft of cool air coming into the drawing room.

She realized she was pacing back and forth. This was ridiculous. It was Stoke who should be fearing her news, not she.

She heard the strong tread of his boots up the stairs.

"Lord Stoke," said the footman.

She turned. Stoke looked so—so rigid. So strong. So powerful.

A claret-colored coat fitted neatly over his shoulders, sloping away from his neck to reveal a pristine white cravat and an understated waistcoat. Always the soldier, wasn't he? Neat as a pin.

Neat enough to make her feel dowdy and embarrassed.

"Please have a seat," she said, intensely aware of the shabbiness of the room, the age of the furnishings. "Would you like some refreshment?"

"No, thank you." His voice was cold and distant, and he made no move to sit down.

She gave the footman a formal smile. "Thank you. That will be all."

The footman gave her a brief bow before backing out the door.

A bow? That had only started recently, hadn't it? Only since Stoke had begun calling on her. Perhaps her association with him had raised her status in the eyes of the servants.

Hoping to appear calm, she seated herself on the hard sofa. "Lord Stoke," she said, "thank you for coming."

His mouth tightened. "You may skip the pleasantries," he said. "I have been waiting long enough for you to explain your intolerable charge against my father. I will not wait any longer."

He was within his rights, she supposed. But she was fiercely reluctant to actually tell him.

She didn't want to hurt him. That was it, wasn't it? As long as he could disbelieve her charge, his pride and his strong sense of honor were undisturbed.

But to admit that his father had done such a thing—that would be a hard blow for a man like him. A man who valued family and duty so strongly.

She clasped her hands together in her lap. "I was fourteen when it happened. A loud noise woke me up one night, and I couldn't figure out what it was. It was raining out, but lightly, and there wasn't any thunder or wind."

She had to make him see how it was, to feel it, even if just a little bit. "I threw on my dressing gown and sneaked out of my bedroom. I could tell the noise was coming from the great hall, so I went to the top of the staircase and tried to see what it was."

She'd been so young then. It was strange to remember that far back, and realize that until that night, she had trusted without question that her father would always protect them from everything, and solve every difficulty that came up.

How much difference one night could make. "It was my father. He'd been in London to take care of some business, and we hadn't expected him back for several days yet. But there he was, in the middle of the night, dripping all over the front hall."

Stoke walked to the window and stared out. She couldn't see his face at all, or have any idea what he was thinking.

She looked down at her hands, trying to concentrate. "I went down the stairs to see what was wrong. He was—he was different. Strange. He'd been drinking, but that wasn't it—he wasn't drunk, and I'd seen him after a few glasses before."

She kept her eyes fixed on her hands. "But his eyes were—confused, lost. Something. He was soaked, but when I came downstairs he hugged me tightly. He was so cold."

Stoke shifted. He probably wanted her to hurry the story. Well, he could learn to wait. "I asked him what the matter was, but he didn't make any sense for the longest time. I realized he'd ridden all the way back from London that night, in the rain. I didn't really know why."

She sighed. "I still don't. I suppose after a great shock, a person doesn't always think straight."

"He'd lost his money, I take it?"

She didn't care for his tone, or his matter-of-fact choice of words. But she knew he didn't want to be here any more than she wanted him here, so she took a deep breath and let her feelings calm. "Yes, he had lost his money. All of it."

"That much is public knowledge." His words were clipped, his voice emotionless.

"Yes, I daresay it is." She hated to think of people gossiping about her family and their lives. "But I don't know how much you know."

He turned away from the window and stared across the room. "As I told you, I know that my father won money from yours, and took horses as at least part of the payment. If you know more, I want to hear it."

He always had to control every situation, didn't he? What had he been like before he was in charge of everyone and everything?

But no matter. "Eventually, my father told me everything. I don't think he told anyone else too much, including my stepmother. And Tom and Louly were just children."

Small children. So easily hurt. "When in London, my father was drawn into a game of whist with your father, Lord Malkham, and a man named Sir Geoffrey Yarrow."

She might as well make this quick. "The game turned into several, and the four men played most of the night. They were at Lord Malkham's townhouse, let me add. When they began, my father was the only one without money troubles. When they finished, the others had his money, and he had nothing."

Stoke pushed away from the window and strode toward her. "That means nothing," he said, leaning down to meet her gaze. "You base your accusation on that?"

"No." She could still hear the rain falling softly on the roof, and her father's boots squelching across the Persian rug. "My father suspected several times that something underhanded was going on. Malkham and Sir Geoffrey guessed what card he held far too often."

"So? That doesn't prove anything."

"Of course it doesn't." She was beginning to lose her temper. "But if you interrupt every two seconds, I'll never get further than the beginning of my story."

He scowled, but remained silent.

Good. "I remember my father telling me that he thought Malkham was behind it all—whatever it was that was going on. The other two kept looking at Malkham in a—a tentative way, I think he said. And he'd known Malkham for years—they were at school together, actually—and he knew that he wasn't trustworthy."

She shook her head. "He never told me, but I suspect my father caught Malkham doing something dishonest when they were young, and . . . well, my father had very clear ideas of right and wrong. Whatever he said or did on that occasion, Malkham never forgave him for it. They were enemies forever after."

Stoke raised an eyebrow. "But your father chose to game with him?"

She sighed in exasperation. "You know what gaming does to people. They don't seem to care whom they play with, or where, as long as the fever is in them. Why else would gaming hells be so popular?"

She nervously rubbed at a spot on her left cuff. "In any case," she continued, "my father was like that. Although he had made a study of probability as it pertained to the cards, when he was in the middle of a game he often ignored logic and went with his instinct. Normally, this led to no great harm."

She shook her head. "But that night, things went against him. He kept losing, and losing. And every time he lost, he thought, 'I can't go home now. I can't face my wife and children and tell them how much we'll have to retrench, and what we'll have to sell to pay the debts.'"

She stared at her cuff. "And so he continued, on and on, always thinking his luck would turn. And all the time having an uneasy feeling about the behavior of his partner and opponents."

"His partner?" Stoke seemed struck. "Who was his partner?"

"Your father."

"But if our fathers were partners in a whist game," he said slowly, "then they were on the same side. If Malkham cheated your father, then he cheated mine as well. So what you're saying makes no sense."

"Yes, it does," she said. "You said yourself your father won a large sum of money from mine. So if they were partners, and yet one lost and one won—what could explain it but cheating? I have no idea exactly how our horses came to be owned by your father—whether he purchased them from my father, or whether Lord Malkham or Sir Geoffrey was an intermediary in some way—but if your father had lost what mine had, he would have been selling his own horses, not buying ours."

She shrugged. "My father lost, your father gained—and there is only one possible reason why. Clearly Malkham and Sir Geoffrey conspired with your father, and paid him for his part in their scheme."

"*Clearly?* I don't think so," he said heatedly. "My father could have played another game against yours, at some other time."

"But he didn't." She clasped her hands together and gazed at him earnestly. "Before the whist game, my father's fortunes were never better. But after, he had lost it all. He immediately came home, and never gambled again, so we know he lost everything that night. You know your father won money along with the other two. You came to that conclusion yourself, didn't you?"

He shook his head and started pacing. "That's not how my father was. He would never have done a thing like that. He had his faults, I admit—who doesn't? But he was a honorable man, and he wouldn't cheat."

"But he did." She hated to say it, but it was the only way. "When my father arrived home that night, he told me that he was certain some sort of trickery had gone on. He said—he said that as he left Malkham's lodgings that night, the last glimpse he had of your father was of him smiling at Malkham."

Stoke wouldn't meet her eyes. "Your father and mine," she continued, "were partners the entire night. If your father had just lost a fortune, he too would have been devastated."

At this, Stoke looked up. "That's your proof?"

"No." She paused for a second. "At first, all my father had were suspicions. He was feverish for days, and just kept raving about—about things. He was a little better after a week or so, and got up, tried to—to carry on. He hadn't worn his overcoat since that night, and when he put it on again—he found something in the pocket. A card."

"A card?"

"A playing card. Your father, it seemed, had special packs of cards made for himself. Instead of having plain white backs, he had the Stoke coat of arms printed on them."

He shifted. "Yes, I know those cards. It was a whim of my father's."

"Well, those were the cards they played with. After the game was over, my father didn't have the money with him to pay his debts, for obvious reasons. So he wrote a promise to pay. He said that sort of thing was common."

"It is."

His voice was uncompromising and hard. "It was their habit, it seems, to bend the playing cards after the game was over, so that they would not be reused. Father said this was a thing many card players did—to make cheating harder. They always played with a new, unbroken pack. And to make sure someone didn't mark the cards and make them look new somehow, they were bent in half."

"Yes, I understand that part," he said impatiently. "But what are you getting at?"

He wouldn't ever forgive her, would he? "My father wrote his promise to pay on one of the playing cards. They were to be discarded, after all. But he accidentally smeared the ink on the first one—he'd had a little bit to drink—and so he rewrote his pledge on a second card. For some reason he put the first card in his pocket."

This was the crux of the matter. "He didn't know for certain he'd been cheated until he found that card. In the brighter light of day, he could clearly see where the card had been marked."

"Marked?" He frowned, his brows jutting out over his dark eyes. "How?"

"I'll show you." She moved over to the mantel and picked up the playing card that lay there. "Here." She moved toward him and held out the card. "See for yourself."

He took the card gingerly, as if it might burn him. He studied the face first. The scarlet ace of diamonds stood in the center of the card, with her father's unsteady writing sloping around it.

Stoke turned the card over. Atalanta didn't even have to look to know every detail of the heraldic shield printed on the back. Three red griffins reared up on a white background covered with black crosses. Separating the griffins was a thick horizontal band of red containing a white lion.

Stoke stared at the card. He tilted it this way, then that, finally walking over to the window to examine it in the brighter light that came through the panes.

"Look at the corners," she told him. "At the crosses, and the claws of the left-most griffin. There are marks there. Made with ink."

He frowned intently at the card, then looked up at her. "This still doesn't prove your argument."

"But can't you see—"

"Yes, I see that the card is marked. I'm not blind. But it does not say who marked the card, or for what purpose. Or who knew about it."

It was perfectly clear, but he just refused to see. "They're your father's cards. Who else could have marked them?"

"But my father had no reason to—to cheat."

She sighed. "I don't know his reasons. I do know that Lord Malkham and Sir Geoffrey were a fair bit older than he—perhaps they persuaded him that such things were commonly done. And I presume he felt he needed the money. You said you were on the Continent then—it wouldn't be surprising at all if you didn't know the full state of your father's finances."

"But I—" He paused, scowling. "I'm sure he wouldn't do a thing like that, no matter how sorely he needed the money."

She raised her hands in frustration. "I have laid all the facts before you. Before that game, my father was wealthy. After that game, he had nothing. And I can vouch for the fact that he did not play your father at any time after he came home that night."

No, she'd known where he was for a long time after that. Ill, bedridden, despairing, when he wasn't sending off their horses or ignoring the men who took the furniture.

"You have the proof in your hand," she said. "The cards were marked—your father's own cards. Your father partnered mine, yet yours won when mine lost. It's really quite simple."

He rubbed at his forehead. "I need time," he said. "I can't think straight just now, so I can't refute you as I should. As I know I *could*."

So that was it, wasn't it? "I'm sorry to have been the bearer of such news, Lord Stoke. But I—" Anything she could say was woefully inadequate. So she just said, "I'm sorry."

He gave her a slight bow, as if they were only formal acquaintances. "I shall take my leave now, Miss James." He paused for a second, then set the playing card down on the mantel. "No one need see me out."

She watched him go. Her chest had a tight pain in it, the way it had when her father had been dying. She knew he would never forgive her, even though he would eventually admit that she told the truth.

But what else could she have done? If she'd never told him the truth, every time she looked at him or heard his name, she would see his father beside him—and her father's memory would not let her have peace.

She crossed to the tall sash window and looked out into the cloudy street. A moment's searching showed her Stoke's tall figure, striding purposefully away. He had been so kind to her.

More than kind. What had he meant by proposing the other night? His sense of duty was fierce, that was certain. He hadn't said anything about love. He hadn't even talked of affection.

But he had talked of money. Oh, how she hated money. If it hadn't been for that, who knew what her life would have been like? Perhaps she would have met Stoke at a random event. Would he have liked her, if he hadn't thought she needed protecting? Would he have courted her, and sent her flowers, and danced with her at balls?

Would he have still wanted to marry her?

She crossed slowly to the worn sofa and sank down on its hard cushions, her eyes staring unseeingly into the cold fireplace. There was no use repining, she knew that. No use wishing things were not as they were. That was what had killed her father, after all, lying in bed day after day, becoming weaker and weaker.

She'd always thought he died because he wished to. Life held nothing for him anymore. He'd broken the lives of those dearest to him, and couldn't face what he'd done.

That was what had set her on this path, of course. Her father had given up, but she would not. She would not leave Tom and Louly to the mercy of the world. When she had finally known in her heart that her father was not going to protect her and her siblings, she had seen her path. She would do what her father could not. She was stronger than him.

She would not abandon Tom and Louly, no matter what it took.

Chapter Fifteen

*T*he Earl of Stoke scowled at one of his father's chaotic account books and cursed his luck. Why had he ever met Atalanta James?

His life had been so simple before that day. He'd had money, position, security—he'd known who he was.

And what his family was.

The Earls of Stoke had always been honorable—hadn't he been telling Edmund that just the other day? And now . . . was it possible that his father had cheated?

He pushed away from the desk and started pacing around the dusty room, hoping it would help him think. Not that he wanted to think.

But he had to. It was his duty.

For a moment he felt like consigning his duty to the devil. He'd never asked to be earl, nor in the least expected it. He wasn't prepared for all it entailed, for preserving the name and ensuring the stability and continuation of the line and the family.

He stared out the window, wishing he were far away, racing across green fields on horseback. Or even in Spain again. Being shot at by cannon was nothing compared to this.

He'd always been so secure in his honor, in his family

name. Things had always seemed so easy before now. Or at least, that was how they looked in retrospect.

He was confronted by an impossible dilemma. Could his father have cheated? Every atom in him screamed to deny it. And yet Atalanta's evidence was strong. And what she couldn't know was just how bad his father's finances had been before his windfall at the tables.

But could that have been enough to drive him to dishonor the family? Surely not.

He turned away from the window and resumed pacing, his head aching. How well had he ever known his father? He had left for the army when he was still a boy. Much of what he knew was from Father's letters, and the occasional scrawl from Cyril or Edmund. So how could he truly know such a thing? Cheating was unthinkable to him—he'd rather die, or have his family bankrupt. Honor was more precious than anything else a man possessed.

But what if his father had felt differently? What if his father had confused honor with the respect in which his family was held?

Look at Viscount James. He had broken no law, kept his word faithfully, and behaved in every way like a gentleman. And yet when the James family became poor, people began to talk as if it were somehow their fault. As if they were the ones without honor.

How could anyone confuse money with honor?

Two days went by without Atalanta hearing anything from Stoke.

She tried to keep busy. She met with Tom to finalize their plans. She wrote a chatty letter to Louly, and a more polite one to the kind Mrs. Knowles, trying to convey how grateful she was. She practiced with the cards, over and over, until spades and hearts circled before her eyes when she lay down at night.

Yet through all of it, Atalanta found herself constantly watching for Stoke. She stared out the drawing room's tall sash windows so often that she knew which of their neighbors threw a penny to the crossing sweepers and which didn't. She peered through her grimy bedroom window until she had memorized the patterns that the dirt made on the glass. When she met Tom in the Park, she had no intention of turning to look at every gentleman who walked by, but she did it anyway. It was ridiculous, she knew—but somehow she couldn't help herself.

On the morning of the third day, as she sat by her bedroom window with a practice game of whist lying neglected before her, she saw him. There he was, striding up the street. From her vantage point, his top hat and coat looked much like any other gentleman's, but she knew his energetic walk, his purposeful bearing.

Her heart beat faster, and she felt suddenly flushed. Which was ridiculous, of course. Why did she have to feel this way, about him of all people? He, who had so much cause to hate her?

She'd made a botch of telling him the truth the other day, that was for certain. But if he was here to talk to her again—if he let her explain everything—if she did it right this time, then maybe . . .

But no, Cousin Harriet was downstairs. They couldn't talk in front of her—that would be disastrous. They wouldn't be able to say a thing.

Much better to meet Stoke out of doors.

Atalanta grabbed her bonnet and pelisse and wriggled into them as she hurried down the stairs. She reached the ground floor, paused to button the front of the garment, and then opened the door just as Stoke was about to knock.

"Good day," she said, a little breathlessly.

Lord Stoke stared for a moment, his tanned face unreadable. "Good day. Were you—were you going out?"

"Yes," she said. But that was a lie, wasn't it? She'd never before noticed how easily she lied. The thought disturbed her. "That is—no. But if you've come to talk to me, I would rather go out than have the conversation inside."

There. That hadn't been too difficult. So why was it her first impulse to say the easiest thing? "We could walk around Mayfair if you like," she said.

He nodded. "Very well."

She closed the tall black door behind her. The breeze was cold against her cheeks, and dark clouds covered the sky, but Stoke didn't seem to notice.

He didn't offer her his arm. She hardly expected it, knowing how he must feel about her. She walked beside him in silence, wishing she could come up with something to say.

"Miss James," he finally said, as they turned the corner onto a quiet street. "I have been thinking about what you told me."

She felt terrible. For a moment she wished she could take back everything she'd said the other day.

But just for a moment. It was better that he know the truth. "Yes?" she said.

Stoke's face was stony, and she knew he was reining back his emotions. "Reluctant though I am to admit it, I concede that the evidence against my father is . . . strong." He swallowed, then took a deep breath. "I fear I have no choice—no choice but to believe that he cheated in that card game."

She hurt for him, for his pain, his humiliation. "I'm sorry," she said. It was totally inadequate, of course. But at least it was true.

"I am someone," he continued quietly, "who tries to do the right thing." His voice was stiff with resolve. "I cannot keep money that was not acquired honestly. So please allow me to repay you the money your father lost."

Good lord. She'd never expected such an offer. "Thank

you," she said, not sure what to say. Not even sure what she felt. "But—but your father wasn't alone. There were three men who won what my father lost. And—and the matter concerns more than money."

"You misunderstand me, Miss James." He took a deep breath. "I shall not only repay you what my father won, but also what Lord Malkham and Sir Geoffrey won. The entire sum your father lost."

She felt stunned. "You—you want to pay it all back? But your father wasn't—he didn't win it all. What about Malkham? What about Sir Geoffrey? Besides, if you pay it all—that's an enormous sum. My God, you cannot be serious."

"And why not?" He stopped walking, and turned to look at her. She could see a glitter in his brown eyes, a tightness in his jaw. "You have made it your life's work to recover the money, have you not? Even if it requires deception. So how can you refuse it when fairly offered?"

"I'm not—" Her head was reeling. "If I take your money, then Malkham loses nothing, neither money nor reputation. Is that your intention? Is that right?"

He frowned at her, his eyes narrowed. "You intend to blacken Malkham's reputation?"

He made it sound like a spiteful act. "His honor is already blackened," she said heatedly. "Why should he bear a spotless reputation after what he's done?"

"Have you ever considered," he said, crossing his arms over his chest, "that if you expose Malkham's cheating, you will point the finger at my father as well?"

That was the heart of the matter. She mustered all her courage, but she couldn't quite look him in the eye. "I don't intend to keep your father's participation a secret."

A thick silence fell between them. She stared at the buttons on his dark coat. Oh, why didn't he say something? The anger radiating from him made her feel weak.

Eventually, she found the courage to look up into his face. His brown eyes were cold—so cold it hurt to look at them. He drew in a slow breath and finally spoke, his voice low. "I beg your pardon. What did you just say?"

How could he make her feel so wrong, when she knew she was right? "Your father cheated," she said, her words sounding thin and weak. "I'm sorry, but there it is. Why should I cover up his sin while exposing Malkham?"

"My father is dead," he said, his voice thick. "What good can it possibly do to ruin his name now?"

She lifted her hands helplessly. How could she make him see? "I just want the truth to come out after all these years."

"Truth? You're a fine one to talk about truth." He leaned closer to her, his rough voice barely above a whisper. "Your whole presence here in London is a counterfeit. Since you arrived you have done nothing but lie, and deceive, and pretend to be anything but what you really are. I thought I knew you, Atalanta. I really did. Stupid of me, wasn't it? I don't know you at all."

He turned away.

Her throat was thick, and her whole body felt cold. "I—I didn't—" What could she say? "I asked you once before—what choices have I? My father was cheated. He was lied to, deceived, and ruined. Three men did that—three men who profited by it, and have never paid the price. Never paid *any* price."

She rubbed her chilled hands together. "After cheating my father, their reputations were better than his. His only crime was trusting—trusting in the honor of those he thought gentlemen. Yet the world calls him a fool, and a— a weak, selfish man—" Her voice broke, but she had to continue. "They call him these things, he who suffered so much. Even his own family—" She paused, swallowed, and drew in breath. "I will not allow that to continue. I cannot. The truth has been denied for too long. And—and whatever you think of me, of what I have done, you know that it pales beside the actions of your father."

"That's not the issue." He stared at the brick wall next to him. "My father is dead. He will never feel the shame of this. But I will, and Edmund, and all my family. My children, too, if I ever have them. Not that I could get any gently bred woman to marry me after such a revelation."

He turned back to her, his eyes dark. "And what joy will you have in that, Atalanta? You've planned your revenge for so long you've forgotten that there are people in this world besides you."

"Revenge? It's not—I'm not trying to get revenge." How could he say such a thing? "I'm trying to provide for Tom and Louly. You've seen them, you know their situations. And if I manage to recover a significant amount of the money, I will be able to give my relatives some of what they should have."

"You're amazing," he said, his voice acid. "All you have to do is open your mouth, and more lies come out. So you're not out for revenge? You just want to provide for your family? The *hell* you do." He glared down at her. "I just offered to pay you everything your father lost. *Everything*. Do you have any idea how much money that is? If you really wanted to provide for your family, you would have accepted my offer. But no, it wasn't good enough, because it didn't include shaming my family before the entire world. On the contrary, you're willing to risk getting nothing at all for your family, as long as you have the chance of tarnishing the names of your enemies." He narrowed his eyes. "It sure as hell looks like revenge from where I'm standing."

He was one to talk. "Perhaps—perhaps that is a little bit of it," she said, her heart pounding. "But what about you? You talk on and on about honor, and honesty, and truth—but when it comes to your family name, you'd rather protect your reputation than let the truth out."

She brushed futilely at a lock of hair that had fallen into her face. "That's what your concern actually is, isn't it? It isn't honor. Your father's honor was gone long ago. Your own honor is not in question." She raised her head high. "What you're trying to protect is your family's status and reputation—not their honor. Or you would be more concerned about righting the wrongs your family committed than covering them up."

He turned away, every muscle rigid. "Is that your final decision?"

If only things didn't have to be this way. "I had planned to recreate our fathers' whist game," she told him sadly, "with you and I as partners, playing against Malkham and Sir Geoffrey. I don't suppose you would ever agree to it now."

He turned back, his expression harsh. "You really thought you could arrange such a thing? And what was I to do—be your puppet?"

"No, I—" Why did it sound so pathetic here in the light of day? "I planned this before I knew you. I didn't plan to tell you any of this."

He scowled. "What could this possibly accomplish?"

She clenched her hands together. "Everyone knows about the night my father lost his estate. If the four of us sat down to a whist game at Lady Isabella's, all eyes would be upon us. All thoughts would be on the game that your father and mine played with Malkham and Sir Geoffrey. If I then made my accusation, and produced the marked card, surely everyone would see the truth."

She gave him a pleading look. "And that's why—that's one reason why—I must expose your father. The marked card was his. There is no way I can expose Malkham without exposing your father, too."

He raised an eyebrow. "You think Malkham would agree

to such a game? And Sir Geoffrey—if he's alive and in London, I'd be surprised."

"Sir Geoffrey lives in an alley off Broad Court, near Covent Garden," she told him. "When Malkham agreed to the game, he also agreed to convince Sir Geoffrey to join us."

When Stoke looked taken aback, she gave a small shrug. "I knew Malkham could not pay me the five thousand guineas in any reasonable amount of time. So he had to agree to another game, hoping to win his money back."

"Do you think he hasn't caught on to *your* game?" He gave her a cold smile. "Do you really think a man as experienced as Malkham didn't notice that you actually know how to play cards?"

"So much the better," she said resolutely. "A man like Malkham, finding himself in such a position, may cheat again. My father suspected he had done so many times. If I catch him at it, it will only corroborate my claim."

He looked at her skeptically. "A mousetrap? I think you'll find Malkham more of a rat than a mouse. And rats can be dangerous."

She didn't need his warnings. What did he think she would do—flee cowering back to the country? "I take it you refuse to help me?"

He widened his eyes. "You must be mad to think you had any chance of winning me over."

She felt cold all over. She'd known this was coming—known from the very beginning—but that didn't make it any easier. She gave a small nod. "That was what I thought. I just—" She swallowed. "I just had to ask." Every part of her ached at the thought of not seeing him again. "I suppose . . . I suppose this is good-bye, then."

He looked torn for a moment—but just for a moment. Then his face hardened. "Very well." With a curt gesture, he indicated the street they had come down. "You clearly know your own way, Miss James, so I will bid you good day. May your luck turn, and all your plans fall to ruins about you."

He turned on his heel and strode away from her, down the narrow street.

When he vanished around the corner, she realized her cheeks were wet with tears. It was all over now, wasn't it? She had lost him. Lost him, just as she always knew she would.

She just hadn't realized how much it would hurt.

Chapter Sixteen

Stoke paced up and down his study, fighting the urge to break things.

Atalanta would be arriving at Lady Isabella's right about now. She would look about her with that inscrutable green-eyed gaze, always collected, always cool. Always pretending.

Yes, that's what it was, wasn't it? Pretense? Her thirst for the cards had been entirely feigned, along with her air of innocence. And everything else, for all he knew. Everything she'd said to him might be a lie.

But . . . it wasn't. He knew that. And if he kept telling himself differently, then he was the one lying.

He sank slowly into his leather chair and stared blankly at his desk. No, he had to admit, Atalanta had rarely lied to him. She had pretended to be worse at cards than she was—though to be honest, he hadn't needed much convincing. When he'd first seen her, it had never entered his mind that she might be as good a player as Malkham or himself.

So in a way, the fault was partly his. Concealing one's hand was an integral part of playing cards, so was concealing one's skill so different?

Had she lied about anything else? He couldn't actually think of an example. Of course, there were things she hadn't told him. Like the fact that his father had won a share of her father's estate. And her plot to recover her family's fortunes by turning cardsharp.

But even after he'd discovered those things, she still hadn't told him that his father had cheated. Come to think of it, she might not have brought it up at all if he hadn't invited Louly to stay with his aunt. Presumably, she had kept that information from him to spare him pain.

But no—did that make sense? Yesterday, she had insisted that she was going to publicly expose his father's cheating. Such news would inevitably come to his ears, she had to know that.

So why hadn't she told him about the cheating sooner?

Had she been trying to delay telling him, knowing that their . . . their friendship, if you could call it that, would be hurt?

But no, that made no sense either. She'd never pursued the friendship, and had often seemed reluctant to continue it. Which, knowing what he now knew, he could understand.

Then what had been her intention?

He stared unseeing at his hands and pondered.

Perhaps . . . perhaps she had never been certain in her own mind whether or not she would actually expose his father? That could be. It made some sense.

But that meant . . . that meant that if he went over to Lady Isabella's now, he might still be able to change her mind.

Atalanta stood nervously at the high-arched entrance to Lady Isabella's opulent drawing room. The atmosphere was thick with candle-smoke and perfume, and she even thought she could smell brandy in the warm, still air.

Yes, still. There was usually much more movement here, wasn't there? Bustling, random movement, the sounds of shuffling cards and jingling coins. But now, everyone seemed strangely quiet. The tables were full as usual, but the players seemed muted somehow.

Glancing about the room, she spotted Lord Malkham first, at his usual table in the corner. And the gentleman across from him, with his back to her—she felt a twinge of relief as she recognized Sir Geoffrey's hunched shoulders.

Everything was ready, then. She hadn't been sure that Malkham had the power to compel Sir Geoffrey to appear, but here he was. As soon as Tom arrived, she could begin the final stage of her design.

But somehow, she felt reluctant to step into the room. Which made no sense. She should be feeling triumphant, or at least . . . determined.

Yet for some reason, she wasn't. Now that the time had finally come, she felt uncertain. She'd spent so many years planning, preparing—studying the mathematics of probability, checking her father's calculations on how this applied to card games. Devising ways to fool her prospective opponents into thinking her stupid, and ways to win their money from them without revealing that she wasn't. So why after all this time was she doubting herself? .

Surely it wasn't the things that Lord Stoke had said.

Stoke could hardly believe he was going to Lady Isabella's. What was the point? He wasn't going to game. He certainly wasn't going to help Atalanta in her lunatic scheme to shame his family. And did he really think he could change her mind, after all his best arguments had failed?

No, not really. But he was going. That much was clear.

He pulled on his greatcoat and nearly snatched his hat out of the footman's hand. Then with a quick stride, he was out the door and climbing into his coach.

He was going to see what happened. That was it. If his name was going to become a byword, he should be there to see it happen. Besides, Atalanta might need his protection.

Now why had that thought come to mind? He wasn't going there to protect her. And she wouldn't thank him for it, either. She'd made it perfectly clear what she thought of him.

No, he would not do a thing to help Atalanta. He just needed to be there.

Atalanta stepped hesitantly into the drawing room, wordlessly accepting a glass of wine offered by a liveried footman. She couldn't take her eyes off Lord Malkham. He looked . . . older today. Perhaps it was the outdated clothes he wore: loose satin breeches and a matching full-skirted, embroidered coat, all in a bright shade of yellow. True, she had never seen him wear the form-fitting fashions that the younger generation favored, and he kept his white hair long, in the style of the previous century. And yet . . . something was different tonight. He looked a full twenty years out of date.

Her father had worn clothes like that. She remembered one embroidered coat quite clearly, and he had worn satin sometimes. Could Malkham intend for her to see the similarity? Did he mean to throw her off her game? If he did, he would hope in vain.

She sipped at her wine, confused by the emotions crowding at her. Memories of her father mixed with thoughts of Stoke, and thoughts of Lord Malkham intruded everywhere. If it hadn't been for Malkham, her father might still be alive, talking and laughing and wearing embroidered coats. If it weren't for Malkham, she and Stoke might . . . might be friends. Or more.

A wave of anger washed over her. She wanted to hurt Malkham. She wanted to hurt him the way he had hurt her father.

But if she did, that would be revenge, wouldn't it?

Suddenly, she no longer understood anything. Why was

exposing Malkham more important than Stoke's happiness? And the happiness of his whole family?

She felt a cold knot in her stomach. Stoke had been right—she was doing this for revenge. Not for Tom, or Louly. What did they care about Malkham's reputation?

No, she was doing it for herself. For the girl she had been, and no longer was. For the humiliation she'd endured as their dining room furniture was hauled off in a cart. For having to grow up too fast, and shoulder the responsibilities that her father found too heavy.

For Minerva. And Icarus. And all their horses, who had been sold like possessions to pay their debts.

If she were truly thinking of Tom and Louly, she'd have taken Stoke's money and forgotten all about how her father was cheated. Could it be that she so hated the thought of losing? Of letting Malkham keep his winnings and his respectability? Of imagining him gloating over the destruction of her father, her family?

Yes, she was out for revenge. She hated to admit it, but it was the truth.

She had always hated how her father had given in too easily, surrendered to his fate without a protest. But did that mean that she had to carry on the fight for all of her life? No matter who it hurt?

She didn't know. She just didn't know.

Stoke strode past the velvet and crystal of Lady Isabella's entrance hall without seeing them.

That tight feeling that he'd had for so long now—could it be guilt? Whatever it was, he didn't like it. He wasn't a hypocrite, in spite of what Atalanta thought. She might think it dishonest to protect his family name after what his father had done, but it was nothing of the kind.

Was it?

He marched up the stairs, his thoughts in chaos. Where

did his duty lie here? To protect his family, and their honorable name? Or to defend honor itself, and let the truth come out? He never thought he'd be questioning the value of honesty. He had always despised a lie more than anything else.

But was that his choice to make?

He paused at the top of the stairs. That was the real issue, wasn't it? Was it his choice to make, or Atalanta's? They both had their duties, or what they believed were their duties, and these were clearly in conflict. Who decided who was right?

He heard a familiar voice in the entrance hall below him. He turned, and there was Tom James, awkwardly handing a hat and greatcoat—both gleaming with newness—to the unflappable footman. The boy then bounded up the stairs, his exuberance at odds with his formal blue coat and starched cravat.

Stoke felt a smile tug at his mouth. "Aren't you a bit young for macao?" he called down.

Tom's face lit up at seeing him, which gave Stoke a surprisingly warm feeling. "Ah, Stoke!" he cried, running up the remaining steps. "You know all the fellows at Eton do nothing but gamble!"

"Forget that I asked. But what are you doing here?" Tom didn't seem the gaming type.

"Have to partner Atalanta, of course." Tom shrugged as much as he could in his tight coat. "Whist isn't exactly my game, but what can you do? Not like we can play Malkham at vingt-un."

Now things made sense. "She bought you those clothes, didn't she?"

Tom shifted awkwardly. "Atalanta figured it would make me look older. I think it just makes me look a fool. Though I don't suppose they'd have let me in wearing my regular togs."

Stoke straightened the bow on Tom's cravat. "There. You look as fine as anyone."

"Thanks." Tom stuck his hands in his pockets and swayed back and forth a bit. "So . . . you aren't sore?"

"Sore?"

"You know—about what Atalanta's doing tonight."

"Oh. That kind of sore." So was he? "I don't know. I was. But—I know how she feels about this. She believes she's doing the right thing."

Tom nodded. "Been planning this forever. Can't tell you how much this means to her. Her father—" He broke off, looking embarrassed. "Well, he was awfully decent. You should have seen her tell off her relatives when they'd run him down, afterwards. They wanted her to blame him, too—say he shouldn't have gamed, that it was his fault." Tom scowled. "She just kept telling them he was cheated, but they never believed her. Never really cared, I don't think."

Stoke's gaze went to the archway that led into the drawing room. "I suppose she's waiting for you."

"Right. Supposed to be here a while ago. Had to fight with the cravat first, though." He ran a finger around the top edge of his stiff neckcloth. "Stupid thing."

Squaring his shoulders, Tom moved toward the archway. Stoke followed him, trying to picture the lad playing whist with Lord Malkham. No doubt about it, the old shark would eat him alive. Admittedly, Stoke had been wrong when he assumed Atalanta wasn't an expert card player, but this was different. Tom clearly didn't have the patience, the cool head, the—the temperament for the tables. Not yet, anyway.

The two of them stepped into the drawing room. Gamesters thronged the tables, in larger numbers than usual. Stoke drew quite a few glances as he entered, and the atmosphere seemed—excited. Anticipatory.

And there stood Atalanta near the entrance, slender and pale, completely alone.

He felt his resolve weakening. His father had hurt her, badly. By his greed and dishonesty, he had torn apart her entire family.

Now Stoke, as the current earl, stood in his father's place. It lay within his power to right that wrong. Could honor be satisfied by anything less?

And how could he turn his back on Atalanta? He loved her. He'd loved her for a long while now, hadn't he? Perhaps it had begun when she'd seen his horses and her face had lit up with joy. Or when she'd taken his hand in the Park. But whenever it had begun, she was his everything now.

Certainty settled on him like a comfortable cloak. The answer was simple. Atalanta had spoken the truth—his father had lost his honor long ago. If Stoke protected his father's reputation now, it would be nothing more than the perpetuation of a lie—the very lie that had so hurt Atalanta.

He knew what he had to do. Ruin his own name. Let the truth come to light.

"Tom," he said. "You can go. I'll partner your sister."

Chapter Seventeen

Atalanta felt Stoke's gaze on her. She turned her head slightly, and there he was.

No wonder his proposal had said nothing about love. How could a man like him love someone like her? Someone hard inside. Unforgiving. Unbending. Someone who would ruin a whole family because of the crimes of one man.

This wasn't right, she realized in a sudden rush of clarity. What was she doing? Seeking revenge, just as Stoke had claimed. Seeking revenge, and calling it justice. Calling it truth.

She couldn't go through with it, she couldn't ruin him. Why had she ever thought she could?

With renewed confidence, she walked over to him. She forced herself to meet his eye, bracing herself for the contempt she expected to see there. But no—his dark eyes looked anything but angry. Somehow, they looked ... warm.

She cleared her throat a bit nervously. "I wanted to tell you—" This should be easy. It was just what he wanted to hear. "I wanted to tell you that—that I'm not going to do it."

Stoke didn't say anything for a moment. He just stared at her, his eyes intense, searching. Finally he shook his head.

"You don't understand. I've changed my mind. I sent Tom away so I can partner you."

She couldn't believe he was saying this. "But—that doesn't make sense." It was so clear to her. "You were right, Stoke. I understand that now. What good could come from blackening your family name?"

A look of frustration crossed his face, followed by reluctant amusement. "I can't believe we're having this argument."

She gave him a rueful smile. "I know. It's rather dizzying, isn't it?" She shook her head. "But all the same, what you said yesterday was quite true. My motive was revenge."

"It doesn't matter if it was."

She gazed at him for a moment, confused. "Of course it does." How could he take this so lightly? And how could he keep looking at her as if she were someone—someone decent, someone worthwhile? "Besides, you've done nothing wrong. Nor has Edmund. Why should you suffer?"

His gaze was gentle. "Why should your family suffer while we live on stolen money and tainted honor?"

"My family doesn't have to," she said earnestly. "You offered to pay back all the money my father lost. That is too much, of course—I would never accept such a thing, the idea is ridiculous—but if you paid back merely what your father won, we wouldn't—" At a sudden gesture from Stoke, she broke off.

"Shall we play?" Malkham's oily voice came from behind Atalanta. "If your lovers' quarrel is quite over?"

As Atalanta turned to face the aged man, she felt Stoke's hand on her shoulder, warm and steadying. "Lord Malkham—"

"We are ready," said Stoke.

Malkham favored Stoke with a brief bow, then led the way to a round table in the center of the room. She tried to catch Stoke's eye, but his gaze was on Malkham's back. The pressure of his hand on her shoulder vanished, leaving her feeling abandoned for a moment. But just a moment, for Stoke took her hand in a warm grasp, his large hand totally engulfing her own. She felt her face warm at the intimacy, here before so many strangers, but Stoke merely threaded her arm through his and led her sedately toward the green baize table.

"Lord Stoke," she said in a low voice, "you understand my position, do you not? I am quite decided."

"I do understand."

But did that mean he agreed? She opened her mouth to ask him, but they had reached the table, and no further discussion was possible.

The room fell strangely quiet. She glanced around briefly, and saw many eyes upon them, bright with curiosity, or perhaps something more. Sir Geoffrey rose from the table in the corner and ambled toward them, muttering to himself.

Malkham pulled out a chair for her, the stiff skirts of his coat rustling as he bent over to grasp hold of it. She hesitated. She didn't know if she could bring herself to sit in that chair just now, with Malkham's withered hands resting on its crimson damask back. And he knew it, didn't he? This was just another attempt to discompose her, to throw her off her game.

Stoke pulled out the next chair as if he didn't see Malkham at all. "Miss James?"

Atalanta gratefully seated herself in the chair Stoke offered. "Thank you, my lord."

Stoke took the seat opposite her. Sir Geoffrey lowered himself heavily into the chair to her left, his thin frame seeming to collapse in on itself even more. He glanced in her direction, his bloodshot gaze not quite meeting hers, and twitched his mouth open in a crooked parody of a smile. Then his face clicked shut again and he stared gloomily down at the table.

"Well, then," said Malkham, his eyes sharp as he settled into the chair next to her. "One hundred guineas per game point?"

As Stoke broke open the pack of cards a bewigged footman offered him, his mind warred with itself. Should he go ahead and reveal his father's dishonor? When he had decided to do so, everything seemed simple—horrible, but simple. So was that the right choice?

Or should he take Atalanta's change of heart as a sign that such a sacrifice wasn't necessary? If even she no longer wanted his family shamed, why in the world should he do such a thing? Or was such a way out a dishonorable course?

He realized he was staring at the pack of cards gripped tightly in his hand, and forced himself to look up. Across the table from him sat Atalanta, her face calm, her eyes anguished. He wanted to hurt Malkham for having done this to her. He wanted to carry Atalanta off somewhere safe, somewhere warm, where he could ease her cares and bring a smile to her soft mouth.

He reined in his thoughts and began shuffling the cards. As always, this gave him an odd sense of calm. The cool smoothness of the card backs, the slight roughness of their edges, felt comfortable in his hands, and the snapping sound of the cards falling into place soothed his jagged nerves.

He continued to shuffle, taking the opportunity it gave him to unobtrusively study his opponents. At first glance, Lord Malkham and Sir Geoffrey Yarrow were two of a kind. Both were elderly—at least ten years older than his father would have been, had he lived—and both wore their long white hair down. But there ended the resemblance.

Malkham was sharp, compact, contained. Every move was tightly controlled, every action carefully planned.

Sir Geoffrey was nervous, distracted, always in motion. His fingers drummed on the table, his neck jerked back and forth, and his mouth moved in a constant silent monologue. His face was as powdered as his hands, and his dark clothes smelled of camphor. Stoke knew he'd never laid eyes on the man before—he wouldn't have forgotten that pale, bony face.

It was hard to imagine his father sitting in his place just five years ago, with Lord Malkham and Sir Geoffrey, about to play a game that would change the lives of all four players so drastically.

This game, too, would decide the fates of four people. But that didn't explain why everyone else in the room stood staring at them as if their own lives depended upon these next few hands of whist.

Hell. They knew all about the game his father had taken part in, didn't they? And they knew that this game was, in effect, a reenactment of the earlier one. That meant gossip. Good, juicy gossip—and if lives were ruined, excellent gossip. Of course, he'd known from the beginning that nothing at Lady Isabella's stayed quiet for long.

With a twist of his wrist, he spread the cards facedown on the green cloth. "Cut for deal."

Malkham won the first deal. Stoke kept a close eye on the cards as the older man reshuffled and dealt them out, but could detect no sleight of hand.

The game soon absorbed all his attention. Atalanta was an excellent partner—knowledgeable about all the conventions, quick to assess the odds, and coolheaded in play. Even better, she seemed to know exactly what he held, and have a fair idea of the distribution between their opponents as well. He knew it must be her years of preparation for this moment, but from time to time he had the eerie feeling that she was reading his mind. He was grateful for her skill, wherever it came from, for he feared he wasn't playing his best. He kept being distracted by her graceful hands, her deft fingers, the way she tossed a card into the center of the table with a flick of her slender wrist.

He had gamed with Malkham before, so the man's assured, subtle play was no surprise. Sir Geoffrey, however, was new to him. After a few hands, Stoke concluded that, despite his agitation, he was a competent player. Stoke had thought at first that the man's increasing restlessness might give clues to what he held, but soon decided the fellow's anxiety had nothing to do with his cards. Perhaps his conscience was chewing at him, over what he'd done to Atalanta's father. Or maybe he feared Atalanta's purpose in bringing him here. Either way, it made no difference to Stoke.

The first few hands went fairly evenly, with Malkham's side winning the first rubber, but taking only two hundred guineas for it. With the second rubber, their luck changed— or perhaps it wasn't luck, but the way Atalanta knew what he was thinking before he even thought it. Whichever it was, by the end of the third rubber he and Atalanta were ahead by a thousand guineas.

While Atalanta shuffled the cards with nimble fingers, Malkham pulled out a jeweled snuffbox. "You play whist well, Stoke." His voice was sly. "You know, you remind me of your father."

Stoke could think of no civil response, so he ignored the man.

Malkham flipped open the ornate lid of the snuffbox and took a pinch of the powdered tobacco inside. "I knew your father well, you do realize. Totally reliable. Always reasonable."

Malkham lifted the snuff to his nose and inhaled. "Afraid I can't say the same for the father of your fair partner."

Atalanta stiffened. Confound Malkham—he was trying to throw her off. "What extraordinary manners you have, Lord Malkham," he said, his voice cold. "You gladly played whist with the late Lord James. You were willing to take his money—all of it, in fact—which he faithfully paid. Then, having bankrupted him, you wait until he's dead and then disparage his memory? I have trouble believing a gentleman would behave in such a way. And you are a gentleman, my lord . . . are you not?"

Atalanta's face was rather red, but her hands stayed steady as they shuffled the cards. Stoke could feel the rising interest of the onlookers, as the emotions of the players rose and scandal became more and more likely.

Malkham closed the lid of his snuffbox with a bony finger. "I meant no offense to the lady, of course."

Stoke let a few seconds go by before he said, "Of course."

Atalanta finished shuffling and set the pack down in front of Malkham with a thump. "Your deal, my lord."

Malkham picked up his snuffbox and replaced it in his pocket. "These cards are too worn, too dirty. I need a fresh pack."

Stoke could see Atalanta's mouth tighten with anger, but no one could object if the dealer called for a new pack. A tall footman set the replacement cards on the table between Malkham and Atalanta. Malkham gave them a brief glance and said, "Please shuffle, Miss James."

Stoke was glad to see Atalanta's face serene as she shuffled the new pack. Malkham surely meant his remarks to discompose her, throw her off her game, and Stoke admired her for foiling Malkham's purpose.

When Atalanta finished shuffling the new pack, she set it firmly in front of Malkham. As Malkham reached for the cards, a sudden exclamation from Sir Geoffrey interrupted them. "Bloody hell!" he shouted, jumping out of his chair. "What is this?"

He was waving his glass of burgundy about, and Stoke waited for it to slosh over onto the luxurious rug. But before more than a few drops splashed out, Sir Geoffrey thrust his glass into the hand of a goggling footman and cried, "Replace that, if you please! Indeed!"

Sir Geoffrey dropped back into his chair, rubbing at his mouth and repeating "Indeed!" over and over, a bit more quietly each time.

When Malkham dealt out the hand and they began to play, Sir Geoffrey subsided for the most part, merely punctuating each trick he took with a quiet, "Indeed." He took a good many tricks, for the luck had shifted, so Stoke had the luxury of hearing that word an annoying number of times.

The cards continued in Malkham's favor. After another two rubbers, Stoke and Atalanta owed their opponents eight hundred guineas. Malkham's dry face actually approximated a smile for once as he surveyed the final trick of the third rubber. "Too bad, Stoke," he said, his voice oily. "But I'm certain your luck will change. In fact, why don't we sweeten the pot? What say you to an extra thousand guineas for the winner of the next rubber?"

Perhaps this was the time to leave gracefully. If Atalanta was not going to accuse Malkham and Sir Geoffrey of cheating her father, then continuing to play only risked what money she'd won from Malkham last time.

He met Atalanta's forthright gaze and gave a slight shake of his head. Her green eyes widened, her mouth tightened slightly, and he realized she was angry.

Angry? At what? More to the point, at whom?

She reached her delicate hand across the green cloth and picked up a card that lay in front of Sir Geoffrey. "Smudges again, I'm afraid. We need a new pack." She dropped the card carelessly in the center of the table and gave Stoke a challenging look. "The new stakes are acceptable to me. And yes, Lord Malkham—I feel sure our luck will change when the cards do."

So that was it. Stoke could barely stop himself from pick-

ing up the card and examining it for suspicious markings.
No wonder the "luck" had so suddenly and sharply changed!

To twice do such a thing as cheat implied, to his mind,
that Malkham had done so many times. Had he no compunction? Or at the very least, no fear of being exposed?

But then, why should he? Having succeeded once, and in
such a large way, might persuade a man that detection was
impossible.

He only wished he knew how Malkham did it. Lady Isabella's footman had brought a new pack—Stoke had seen
Atalanta break the tax seal before shuffling them. Surely
Malkham had not found a way to mark a pack of cards, then
reseal them? Such a step would not only be nearly impossible, but would be a crown offense as well. And even if
Malkham could do such a thing, how could he then arrange
for the cards to be in Lady Isabella's possession?

No, that wouldn't work. And he didn't see any way for
Malkham or Sir Geoffrey to have marked the cards after
Atalanta broke open the seal.

Which left only . . . what? How in the hell had Malkham
marked a sealed pack of cards?

Atalanta stared at the tax seal on the new pack of cards in
her hand. There was no way to rip the seal open and then
piece it back together like new. So how had Malkham done it?

And more importantly, would he be able to do it again?

She broke the seal in half and unwrapped the cards. Fan-
ning them out before her, she studied the plain backs. Their
pristine white reflected the golden candlelight back at her.
Definitely unmarked.

She straightened the pack and set it quietly in front of Sir
Geoffrey. "Your shuffle."

Sir Geoffrey's bloodshot eyes avoided hers. "Indeed," he
muttered under his breath. "Indeed."

She had no idea what to do. If Malkham managed to

mark the cards again, how could she prove it? She could show the card, certainly, and perhaps the patterns of dots and smudges would convince the onlookers that the cards were marked, but who could say who had marked them? Any of the four of them could have done it.

At a loss, Atalanta looked across the table at Stoke. His brown eyes were warm, and he gave her such a smile that for a second she forgot where she was. His gaze was so strong and steadying, she felt as if she had suddenly been turned right side up.

Of course. Why did she keep assuming she was alone in all this? Stoke was with her. If she didn't think of what to do, Stoke might. If something went wrong, she wasn't the only one it would affect, nor the only one who would be fighting to fix it. Stoke would share any win or loss that she had— he was her partner.

She smiled gratefully back at him, feeling a strange joy bubbling up in her chest. She didn't know why he should make her feel so strong, so confident, so safe, but he did. And somehow she knew that everything would be all right.

When Sir Geoffrey handed the cards to him, Stoke realized he was just sitting there, staring at Atalanta. He might as well shout out loud how he felt about her. For some reason, that sounded tempting.

The game resumed. Malkham and Sir Geoffrey won the next hand by a small margin, but the hand after that went very well for Stoke and Atalanta. Their luck had indeed changed—with the change of the pack, of course.

As Stoke collected the cards and put them in front of Malkham to shuffle, the elderly peer pulled out his snuffbox again.

By God. That was it.

Stoke examined Lord Malkham's antiquated coat. "I've never seen you dress like that, Malkham," he said in a loud, clear voice. "Your coat is . . . unexpected, wouldn't you say?"

Malkham gave him a narrow-eyed glance. "Your point?"

"My point?" He pushed back his chair and stood up. "Lord Malkham, I request that you turn out your pockets."

Malkham set down his snuffbox with a thump. "I beg your pardon? I know I cannot have heard you aright."

"You heard me." The crowd around them pulled closer, murmuring in excitement. "Lord Malkham, I *demand* that you turn out your pockets."

Instead, the man picked up his snuffbox again, opening the lid with a flick of his thumb. "Do you realize what you're saying, Lord Stoke?" Malkham's hand shook slightly as he took a pinch of snuff and snapped the lid closed again.

Atalanta gracefully rose to her feet. "Lord Malkham," she said, her voice smooth but cold, "You have been asked to show what is in your pockets. As a gentleman, you must do so."

Malkham thrust his snuffbox back into his coat pocket. "Nonsense, girl. Nonsense. You don't know what you're saying." Steadying himself on the table, he stood slowly. "I refuse to play cards with anyone who shows such a lack of breeding."

Atalanta held her head high. "You must turn out your pockets, my lord."

Malkham bared his teeth. "Just like your father, aren't you? Such a sanctimonious, smug, holier-than-God, cowardly little prig was Augustus James, and you—"

Stoke put a heavy hand on Malkham's shoulder. "If you do not immediately empty your pockets, I will do it for you." He glanced meaningfully at the people crowded around them. "And if I do not, I see there are many here who will gladly take my place."

Malkham sneered and turned away. But before he could

take a second step, he was surrounded by stony-faced gentlemen.

So that no one could later claim any trickery, Stoke allowed the men around Lord Malkham to empty his pockets. And sure enough, these contained two open packs of cards—one marked, one not.

Stoke examined the cards. "It took me a while to figure out what you were doing, Malkham," he said, giving the man a contemptuous glance. "You buy cards of the same type that Lady Isabella uses. You mark them, and bring them here in the voluminous pockets of your ancient coat. You substitute them for the proper cards when it is your turn to shuffle, using your snuffbox as an excuse to reach into your pocket. I take it Sir Geoffrey's odd behavior was to distract our attention at the critical moment?"

He turned to see Sir Geoffrey's reaction, only to realize that Malkham's partner had given them the slip.

Chapter Eighteen

$\mathcal{F}$ive minutes later, Atalanta escaped the chaos in the drawing room and hurried down the grand staircase. She had hoped to find Tom waiting for her in the opulent hall below, but there was no sign of him. The whist game had seemed to fly by, but she supposed it had actually taken a fair while.

Perhaps Tom was outside? A footman in blue livery held the stately front door open for her as she darted out to check.

Sure enough, she found Tom sitting on the front steps, asleep. "Tom." She waved to the footman that he could close the door behind her. "Tom, wake up."

She stood on the step below him and shook his arm gently. "Tommy, we won!"

His eyes half opened and he murmured something. He always had been slow to wake up.

"Tom. Tom! We won." She continued to shake his arm. "We won, Tom. Everything's all right now. Lord Stoke came through. He saved us, Tom. Everyone knows Lord Malkham is a cheat. We won, Tom."

Tom jerked awake. "What?" He sat up, groaning a little. "Atalanta? We won?"

She knew she had a huge grin on her face. "We won, Tom. Malkham and Sir Geoffrey cheated again, and Lord

Stoke caught them—they're shunned men now. No one will play with them—no one will even talk to them after tonight. Not that Sir Geoffrey is likely to mind that, but—"

Tom rubbed at his eyes. "Well done! I knew you could do it! So, what about Stoke? Does everyone know what his father did?"

"No. And I think that's for the best," she said firmly. "Some of them may deduce the truth, but what really matters is that Lord Malkham is finished." She wrapped her arms around herself. "Aren't you freezing out here?"

Tom lumbered to his feet. "Anyone who's slept in an Eton dormitory never feels cold again."

In the lamplight, Atalanta could see that Tom's smart new clothes had suffered the expected fate. "Perhaps soldiering is not the best career for you after all," she said, moving around him to brush the worst of the dirt off the back of his coat. "I believe officers are expected to be neat."

Tom rolled his eyes. "Not on campaign."

"Tidy kit. Clean pistol. Shining carbine. Gleaming horse."

"I can do the horse part," he said, "but the rest of it—"

"Is quite true," came Stoke's voice from behind her. "Listen to your sister—she speaks wisely."

Atalanta turned and saw Stoke standing on the top step. "Now you've done it," she told him with a laugh. "Nothing is less likely to be obeyed than 'listen to your sister.' "

"That would be unfortunate," said Stoke. "By the way, Atalanta, you forgot your pelisse."

She realized he held her well-worn garment over his arm, and that he wore his greatcoat and hat against the cold. "Oh, I—thank you. I hadn't meant to leave yet, you see."

Tom extended his hand to Stoke. "Thank you for helping us," he said, as the earl took his hand in a firm grip. "So why don't you think I'd be a good officer?"

"A waste of your talents. Wouldn't you rather breed horses?"

"Wouldn't I—good God, yes! Are you offering me a position?"

"I am. I take it you are interested?"

"Rather!"

Stoke laid his hand on Tom's shoulder. "I'll be glad to have you. We can work out the details tomorrow—you look half asleep."

"I am half asleep." Tom grinned at Atalanta. "Good work, sis. Don't stay up too late." He gave them a jaunty wave and set off down the street.

Atalanta watched Tom's bedraggled figure until he turned the corner. She felt hopeful about him for the first time in a long while.

And it was all due to Stoke. She felt the earl's warm presence beside her, and wanted to turn and thank him, but a sudden awkwardness descended upon her.

"Do you prefer to freeze?" Stoke finally asked, his voice low.

Then she did look at him. He smiled, but his dark eyes were serious. "I suppose I am cold," she said, noticing for the first time that she was shivering.

"Here." Stoke unfolded her blue pelisse and held it open for her. "Let me help you."

She guided her hands into the sleeves, and pulled the soft fabric up her arms and over her shoulders. His hands lingered for a moment, his breath warm on the back of her neck, and she had a sudden urge to put her hands on his and pull him closer.

Instead she fastened the front of the pelisse. "Thank you," she said. "I don't suppose you got my bonnet as—"

"Of course." He handed it to her.

He placed it over her braids, and her cold fingers needed three attempts to tie the ribbons beneath her chin. "I—I wanted to thank you, Lord Stoke. I—"

"Don't thank me."

"But I—"

"Please." He held his arm out. "Will you walk with me?"

She hooked her arm through his, and they set off slowly down the street. She was surprised to see the sky lightening to the east. Had their game been that long? "Do you know what time it is?"

Stoke patted her hand. "Don't worry. It's early yet."

She looked up at him to argue, and saw a twinkle in his brown eyes. "I suppose it is. And my cousin complains I'm never up in the morning."

They strolled up the street in the uneven light provided by the streetlamps. When they reached the broad expanse of Stanhope Street, Stoke turned eastward. "Miss James," he said. "Atalanta. I believe you left Lady Isabella's before affairs were quite finished."

"I'm sorry—"

"No, no. I just wanted to assure you that Malkham is quite thoroughly ruined. Socially, that is. Sir Geoffrey too, though I doubt such an eccentric will notice the difference."

"I think he is rather mad."

"Not so mad he couldn't conspire to cheat you again. Cheat us."

"True."

They walked in silence for a few moments. "As to the money," Stoke eventually said, "both men come from prominent, wealthy families. I expect the Malkhams and Yarrows are likely to pay their relatives' debts of honor to preserve their own reputations. It only remains to be seen whether they make redress merely for tonight, paying what we ought to have won in a fair game, or whether they include your father's game as well. Anyone there tonight with a grain of intelligence must realize the game five years ago was fraudulent, so I have hope that they will."

Atalanta looked up at his shadowed face. "If they realize

it was false, then they might blame your father as well. I'm sorry for that."

"I'm not." Stoke smiled softly down at her. "What's past is past. As long as my own actions are honorable, I'll hold my head high. And—there are far worse things than scandal."

They approached the end of the street, and Hyde Park lay before them, gray and green in the dawning light. "It's so still," Atalanta said. "I've never seen it so still before."

"And no traffic to worry about." Stoke led her across deserted Park Lane toward the black iron railings of Stanhope Gate. "Ah. I had hoped the Park would be open this early. Nothing like an early-morning stroll."

"Or a late-night stroll?" asked Atalanta.

"Definitely morning. Late night is tired, furtive, dangerous. Early morning is—fresh. Clean."

"You aren't tired?"

Stoke turned to face her, and the rising sun made his face glow. "How can one be tired on such a morning?" He led her forward, along the footpath toward a stand of hawthorn trees. "You seem remarkably calm under the circumstances."

"Under the circumstances?"

Stoke drew her into the quiet grove. The spring leaves on the trees were just beginning to look green, and their clusters of white blossoms were clearly visible in the pale light. Atalanta felt cut off from all the world. She was alone here with Stoke, in private. She felt a slight shiver run up her arms, and it wasn't from the cold.

She turned and looked toward the east, where the slate roofs of Mayfair formed dark outlines against the brightening sky. "And what circumstances would those be?"

Stoke moved beside her, and she could feel his eyes on her. "In this one night, Atalanta, you have changed from impoverished orphan to wealthy heiress. You will have the money my father won from yours, and almost certainly money from Malkham and Sir Geoffrey as well—or at least from their families. You can do as you wish now. You are free."

With his words, the truth sank in. She was free. For the first time since her father's death, she could do what she wanted, be whom she pleased. It was a dizzying feeling.

Atalanta watched the sky over London growing brighter every second, and heard the birds in the trees around them chattering away. Part of her was cold, but somehow the smell of the dew-damp grass warmed her inside with its vigor, its life.

"Thank you," she said quietly. She turned and looked at Stoke, at his brown eyes so bright in the rising light, the slow smile that lit his whole face. "Thank you, Stoke. For everything."

His eyes grew serious. "That sounds suspiciously like good-bye."

"No!" She was embarrassed by the emotion in her voice. "That is—that wasn't how I meant it."

"Good." He paused for a second, looking uncertain. "Atalanta, I—Miss James—Atalanta—"

He caught her eye, and they both laughed. "I think you can call me Atalanta by now," she said. "My sister's living with your aunt, you're hiring my brother, we've been partners in conspiracy—"

"And whist."

"And whist. We're practically family."

He gave her a steady look. "If you start calling me Brother, I'm leaving."

"I'm not—I didn't mean—"

He stepped toward her, taking her hands in a firm grip. "Atalanta, I'm not asking if you feel the same way I do, I'm just—I just—"

She took a deep breath, willing her heart to stop pounding. "What way is that?"

Stoke's eyes grew darker. "Ever since I met you, you've

haunted me, Atalanta James. When you're not with me, I can't get you out of my head. You're—" He reached up a hand and softly touched her cheek, then brushed his fingertips lightly against her throat. "You're driving me mad. Especially when you look at me like that."

Atalanta swallowed. "Like . . . what?"

"Like you want me to kiss you."

Atalanta opened her mouth to say yes—or no—or *something*, but no sound came out.

"Do you?"

"Do I?" she echoed dazedly.

Stoke tilted her face up gently. Slowly he untied the ribbons beneath her chin and pushed her bonnet back, then cradled her face in his hands. His first kiss was soft, hardly a touch at all. The second was longer. By the third kiss, Atalanta had to grab on to the front of his coat to keep her balance.

"Oh, Atalanta," he breathed against her lips. His kiss grew more urgent. He wrapped an arm around her waist and pulled her against him, his mouth seeking, impatient. Atalanta melted against him, wanted him to press harder, wanting—oh, so much.

"Atalanta," he finally murmured against her mouth. "Atalanta, you have to marry me after this, you know. You can't do this to a man and then leave him unless you mean to drive him mad."

Atalanta was so besieged by strange yearnings that it took a moment for his words to sink in. "You—you want to marry me?"

"Of course I do. God, Atalanta, how could you expect me to live without you?"

"But . . ." She pulled away slightly, trying to order her chaotic thoughts. "I'm not sure you even know me—not really."

"How can you say that?"

She'd spent years suffering, after her father had acted

without thinking. She couldn't do that to Stoke. Steeling herself, she placed her hands flat against his chest and pushed him away. "You don't. Really, you don't."

He let her go immediately, a frown on his face. Suddenly cold, she wrapped her arms around herself. "Listen," she said gravely, gazing up into his frustrated eyes. "I'm not—I'm not what I should be. I didn't realize it until yesterday." How could she explain this nebulous feeling? "For years I've—I've hardly thought of anything else but the card game, and how to make things right. I never thought about what I was doing to myself. But when you said I was just out for revenge—well, I didn't want to believe it. I *didn't* believe it—not at first."

He raised a hand protestingly. "I was wrong."

"No, you were right. I *was* out for vengeance, though I had a hard time admitting it to myself. Yes, I was also doing it for Tom and Louly—especially Louly. And to try to save my family from the—the taint of having been ruined by a wastrel. And though my relatives have perhaps not done their best by Louly and me, I also wanted to restore to them what should have been theirs."

"Of course your motivations were complex, Atalanta." His voice was rough with emotion. "You're a human being."

"But there's more. Stoke, I spent the last five years of my life planning revenge. Can you see what that means? I schemed to ruin people's lives—even though some of them did not deserve it."

Oh, why couldn't she explain it right? She clenched her hands in frustration. "I practiced and plotted and—and that does something to you inside. I'm not the person I once was. I'm not the person I could have been. So what kind of wife would that make me? I've learned to push down my emotions if they get in the way of my goals. I'm cold, Stoke. Cold inside. Shouldn't a woman be warm?" Her voice broke on the last word, and she stopped, overwhelmed.

"You are warm." He took her in his arms and pulled her close against him. "I saw you with Louly. I've seen you with Tom. You haven't lost any of your warmth, or your love. I knew that when I saw you go into raptures over Lucifer and Rogue." He smiled down at her. "If two horses can bring that out in you. . . . Atalanta, the girl you were isn't dead. She's part of you." He reached up and brushed a stray wisp of hair off her face. "And yes, you have learned to be hard when you need to—but that's not a bad thing." He tucked the hair behind her ear, then stroked his thumb down her cheek. "I admire your ability to do what you believe is right, even if you have to fight yourself. That's—that's what honor is, I think. And whether or not your choices were perfect doesn't change a thing."

He thought her honorable. He, who had risked his life for his country, who treasured honor above all else. The thought humbled her.

And she did have warmth in her, didn't she? What she had said about herself might be true, but it wasn't the whole truth. "Do you—do you really think you could be happy with me as your wife?" she asked with dawning hope. "A woman who was once a cardsharp?"

"As long as you play an honest game from now on." His dark eyes glinted at her. "And no thousand-guinea wagers— my heart couldn't stand it. But somehow I suspect that won't be a problem."

She gave him a rueful smile. "I'm sorry I let you think I was a dedicated gamester. I do love the cards, but I'm just as happy playing for nothing." Her smile turned into a grin. "Though I admit it was rather fun to capot you."

"You can capot me again if you like," he said, his voice husky. "In fact, you can do all sorts of things to me. But not if you don't marry me." His eyes grew serious. "I love you, you know."

She felt tears gathering in her eyes. "I love you, too. Desperately." She reached up and touched his cheek. "And yes, if you truly want me, then nothing would make me happier than marrying you."

His arms tightened around her. "Kiss me."

She ran a finger lightly over his mouth, then reached upward and touched her lips to his. She wound her arms around his neck and held him close as he kissed her lovingly.

"And, of course," he said, sprinkling kisses across her face, "we shall have Louly live with us. And Tom, as long as he wants."

She felt a warm glow build inside her. "I don't know what I ever did to deserve you, Stoke."

He dropped a kiss on her nose. "I think you know me well enough to call me Richard by now. It's not as exotic as Atalanta, but it's all I have."

"Richard." She smiled up at him. "I think the name suits you. Richard the Lionheart."

"So, soon-to-be Mrs. Lionheart, more formally known as Lady Stoke, I've been wondering one thing." He gave her a quizzical look. "Do you, or do you not, think you can beat me at a fair game of piquet?"

She grinned up into his twinkling eyes. "Is that a challenge, my Lord Stoke?"

"I believe it is, my fair Lady Gamester."

The sun's rays broke through the craggy hawthorn branches, bringing a misty glow to the white flowers all around them. With a happy sigh, Atalanta savored the moment. "Then I am delighted to accept."